FITZWILLIAM DARCY, GUARDIAN

A PRIDE & PREJUDICE VARIATION

JENNIFER JOY

Published by Jennifer Joy

Facebook: Jennifer Joy

Twitter: @JenJoywrites

Email: contact@jenniferjoywrites.com

Sign up for my Historical Romance New Release Newsletter for the latest news about my books and additional scenes!

ISBN-13: 978-1-944795-28-3

CONTENTS

CHAPTER 1

PEMBERLEY SEPTEMBER 1812

"Come, Darcy. Is there nothing I can say to change your mind?" Charles Bingley pleaded, his usual light-hearted manner replaced with somber candor. It ought to have added more weight to his invitation.

But Fitzwilliam Darcy would not budge.

Darcy shook his head, fingering the black band around his coat sleeve. "I am honored you wish to include me, Bingley, but I must beg your patience. I cannot leave Pemberley. Not yet."

Bingley set down his drink. Clasping his hands together, he leaned forward. "You have not left Pemberley in a year."

"Nine months," Darcy corrected. Nine endless months that had passed as quickly as a breath now that they were gone.

"A difference of three months does not make your isolation any better. You have shut yourself off from the world. It is not good."

Were Darcy to relive the past months again, he would still have acted exactly as he had done. There had been no other option.

Bingley added, "Is this how your dear sister would wish for you to live after—?"

Darcy's eyes snapped to Bingley, who bit his lips together and shrank back in his chair. He did not say the word aloud, but it loomed in the air. Bingley did not know the half of it, nor could Darcy tell him. There was no time to mourn, nor would Darcy share what was his alone to bear.

"I thank you for your concern, Bingley," Darcy replied, reaching for his brandy when his throat tightened. Tossing back the contents of his glass, the burn a welcome reprieve, he added, "Georgiana always wanted the best for the ones she loved."

Deep breath. Her name was still difficult to say aloud when she was not there to reply to it. Another breath. "However, it has only been two months since she was laid to rest. I am not ready to go out into society."

Bingley shook his head. "Two months, two years, two decades. Grief will take all the time you give it. You must live, Darcy. It is not only the time your sister has been gone, but the months you have spent in her care until consumption claimed her."

Darcy gritted his teeth together. He despised lies. He detested liars. And yet, that was what he had become.

"Truly, you are to be commended," continued Bingley. "There are few brothers as dutiful as you have proved to be. But I worry for your health if you continue in this same attitude. Come. Join me and my sisters in Hertfordshire."

The undeserved praise stung. Not one day passed without Darcy wishing he could turn back time. He would not have trusted when he needed to protect. He would not have been too late. But as much as he wished to control time, he could not reverse it. Nor had he managed to extract Bingley from his parlor, though he had refused his offer many times.

Perhaps Bingley would stop insisting if Darcy showed a measure of consideration. "Hertfordshire?" Darcy asked politely.

His normal enthusiasm restored, Bingley spoke excitedly, "Yes. You will recall how I had wished to let an estate near a village called Meryton. It was a year ago."

Darcy remembered. Bingley had asked for his opinion and guidance, and Darcy had been agreeable to the idea. The day before his departure to meet Bingley, Georgiana had shown up in Pemberley's entrance hall, sopping wet, gaunt, and expecting George Wickham's child. That had been nine months ago.

Reaching for his glass only to see it was empty, Darcy cleared his throat. "I had hoped you would continue your plans without me."

Bingley colored. "I ought to have gone, but I did not trust myself to manage an estate without the benefit of your experience. My dependency reflects poorly on my character, I realize, but it is the truth."

Why did Bingley not leave? He deserved better company than this. "I did not mean to chastise you, Bingley, only to appease my conscience for not accompanying you."

"I do not fault you for putting your sister's needs ahead of my own. Had you acted otherwise, I would have felt horribly selfish and guilty." Taking another sip of his drink (two more and he would be done, calculated Darcy), Bingley continued, "Do not blame yourself. I was not ready for the responsibility I would have to bear if I were to do a proper job of it. Had I gone alone then, I would have made a muddled mess of everything, I am certain." He chuckled softly, perfectly at ease with his faults.

Darcy envied him. He could not afford to have faults. Not when his last failure had cost Georgiana's life.

She had married over the anvil at Gretna Green. Darcy's little sister, of whom he was entrusted guardianship, had signed her death sentence when she wrote her name beside a ne'er-do-well out to get her fortune. Wickham had killed her.

But Darcy's oversight had made it possible.

Bingley's happy tone clashed against Darcy's dark turn of mind.

"You can imagine my surprise when I heard the property was still empty, and so I did what I was not ready to do a year ago." Bingley's chest puffed out as he announced, "I let Netherfield Park. I have a good feeling about the place, Darcy. Think of the new people we could meet and the countryside we can explore and hunt on. The property is extensive, with three lakes." He listed all the attributes in such a way as to entice Darcy to agree to his proposal.

Holding up his hand before Bingley was carried away in his own excitement, Darcy said, "I thank you, but my reply remains unchanged. I cannot leave."

Bingley opened his mouth — no doubt to

continue in his fruitless exhortations — but Mrs. Reynolds entered the parlor then. Her hands were clasped in front of her; her shoulders, hunched up to her ears.

Darcy tensed. Steadying his breath, he asked, "What is it Mrs. Reynolds?"

She met his eyes, and he felt the intensity in her firm look. "I apologize for the interruption, Mr. Darcy, but there is a situation which requires your immediate attention."

Her vagueness could only mean one thing.

Rising, Darcy bowed to Bingley, who had sense enough to know their call had come to an end.

"I hope you change your mind, Darcy. You are always welcome in my home, be it in London or Hertfordshire," he said.

It felt awkward to smile, but Darcy gave it a try. "Thank you, Bingley. I appreciate the invitation, though I cannot accept it," he said, leaving the room with Mrs. Reynolds while the butler saw to his friend. Darcy spared him no more thought, his entire focus consumed with the matter at hand.

Wordlessly, Darcy and the housekeeper walked up the stairs.

Hearty wails echoed down the hall, growing louder as they reached the fourth door.

"Whatever ails her, it is not her lungs," Mrs. Reynolds said as she stepped aside for Darcy to pass.

Mrs. Bamber paced the room, the inconsolable child defying the wet nurse's efforts to calm her.

Securing the door behind him, Darcy rushed over to the babe Mrs. Bamber thrust into his arms. "What is my little girl upset about?" he cooed, settling his anxious charge against his shoulder and rocking back and forth until he felt her body relax.

Mrs. Bamber rubbed her eyes, her hair frizzing out around her plump, ruddy face. "I am sorry, Mr. Darcy. I could not calm her no matter what I did. She was determined to have you."

Pulling a chair closer to the fire with his free hand, Darcy said, "You know I will always come when Anne needs me. Pray rest, Mrs. Bamber, and tell me why she is out of sorts. She is not ill, I hope?" Darcy's hand spread over Anne's back protectively, his stomach twisting.

With a sigh, Mrs. Bamber looked up at him. "She is a healthy child if ever I saw one, Mr. Darcy. That is not the problem."

"What is it, then?" he pressed.

Mrs. Bamber looked at Mrs. Reynolds, only continuing when the housekeeper nodded. "You will not approve of what I must suggest."

"Say it all the same. There is nothing I will not do to protect my sister's child."

Mrs. Bamber took a deep breath. "She needs to be around other people. She needs to leave this house — as do you, if I may be so bold." She gestured toward the closed curtains. "I dare not show Baby Anne the beauty of her own surroundings lest she is discovered. It is a pity."

She was right, of course, but what she suggested was impossible.

Mrs. Reynolds moved closer to the nurse, stopping once she stood in line with Mrs. Bamber's chair and giving Darcy the impression that he was in a battle where he was outnumbered. She said, "We cannot keep the baby a secret forever. We have no recourse."

Indeed, it was a fact of which Darcy was also well aware. But he refused to accept it. "Anne is under my protection and care. I will not go back on my promise."

Anne's little fingers gripped around the fold of Darcy's cravat, and he heard her yawn. Closing his eyes, he rested his cheek against her fuzzy head. Softly, he said, "I expect to hear from Mr. Rochester soon. If there is a way I can adopt Anne or keep her as my ward, he will find it. I will do what is required." Mr. Rochester was his last hope. Darcy had exhausted every other resource.

Pursing her lips together in her thoughtful way, Mrs. Reynolds said, "I could not help but overhear Mr. Bingley's invitation. You have relatives in Hertfordshire, do you not, Mrs. Bamber?"

The wet nurse's eyebrows creased. "Yes, I do, and I know them almost as intimately as my own children, thanks to my cousin. She writes often and extensively. Madeline Bamber she was. Madeline Gardiner she has been for several years now. Her husband's sister resides in Hertfordshire."

Darcy did not like the manner with which Mrs. Reynolds pinched her chin and considered him.

She said, "I remember Mrs. Gardiner. Her father had the shop in Lambton. You may not remember him, Mr. Darcy, as you were young when they left for London. He was an honest man, and your own mother was known to converse at length with his daughter. Lady Anne was an exceptional judge of character."

Where was she going with this reasoning?

She continued, "I believe we both know what Mr. Rochester will say. Can you not help yourself along, Mr. Darcy? Especially when you have already received an invitation from Mr. Bingley?"

Darcy's jaw dropped. She would have him marry

while he was still in mourning and when Anne clearly needed him? She would have him leave Pemberley, endangering Anne?

"Absolutely not," he hissed, covering Anne's ear for fear of disturbing her.

Mrs. Reynolds asked Mrs. Bamber, "Are your relatives in Hertfordshire the sort of people to be trusted with our charge? Are they as sensible as Mrs. Gardiner was known to be?"

Had she not heard him?

Mrs. Bamber looked between the two of them, answering when Mrs. Reynolds encouraged her with another nod. "The mother is a nervous, flighty creature. I would not trust her with a puppy, much less with our sweet Anne. Their father's estate is modest, and I know it is a source of anxiety to him that it is entailed to his nearest male relation. He has five daughters, you see, and only recently did the youngest marry … and she to a militia officer without two pennies to rub together."

This questioning served no purpose. Darcy had already refused Bingley's offer. He turned to the wall where a portrait of Georgiana hung, turning Anne so she could see her mother while Mrs. Bamber expounded on the subject of her Hertfordshire relatives.

"However, my cousin Madeline always speaks

highly of the two eldest Bennet daughters. She has nothing but the kindest things to say about them, and Madeline is nothing if not sensible and steady, as you recall."

"They are daughters of a landed gentleman?" Mrs. Reynolds asked. Darcy felt her eyes on his back. He refused to turn around.

"Yes. They are proper ladies," Mrs. Bamber said with pride.

Darcy eyed the door connecting the nursery to his bedchamber. He had learned over the past couple of months to carry out several activities with only one arm, and there was a book on his desk he would much rather read than endure the present conversation. He took a step toward the door, but Mrs. Reynolds swooped around him to block his path.

With a sweet smile directed at the sweet blossom in his arms, Mrs. Reynolds planted herself between Darcy and his escape. She was a clever one who knew him too well.

He was trapped.

Wasting no time, Mrs. Reynolds asked Mrs. Bamber, "What else can you tell us about your two eldest nieces?"

If anything, Mrs. Reynolds made him more determined than ever to stay on at Pemberley. The last place in the world he would ever agree to travel would be to Hertfordshire. She could stare at him all she wanted. His answer would remain unchanged.

"Miss Jane Bennet is the eldest, and a real beauty she is reputed to be. She has a way with children, and Madeline praises her calm manners," said Mrs. Bamber.

Darcy pretended he did not notice the look Mrs. Reynolds gave him at that. He would not leave Anne, and that was final.

Continuing, Mrs. Bamber said, "Miss Elizabeth is the second daughter. She is a clever one, but she is not cruel or greedy. When the heir to her father's estate proposed marriage last year, she refused him, stating that they could never be happy together."

"She put her own happiness ahead of her security and that of her family?" Darcy asked. He was not impressed. What he would give to secure Little Anne's future!

Bowing her head, Mrs. Bamber mumbled, "I thought it was romantic. Her father is — or at least he was at the time — in good health. I suppose he is unchanged. I have not heard from Madeline yet this month. But, Lizzy, as Madeline calls her in her letters, has youth on her side. She was not yet of age when her cousin proposed. I cannot say she would react the same if a handsome young gentleman with kind manners and a gentle heart were to cast his eye in her direction." The way Mrs. Bamber looked askance at Darcy as she spoke left little doubt to whom she referred.

Was he to be reduced to heeding the machinations of two females in his employ?

"I will not travel to Hertfordshire to propose marriage to an absolute stranger," Darcy said bluntly.

Mrs. Reynolds replied snappily, "If your only recourse is to marry and produce an heir before Wickham finds out about his daughter, then I would encourage you to join Mr. Bingley in Hertfordshire. Like it or not, you will have to enter society again. You must marry! You could hardly do better in society. All of your acquaintances know Mr. Wickham, and he would sooner turn their sympathies against you."

Darcy was well aware of the difficulties without Mrs. Reynolds pointing them out to him. While he had been busy caring for his sister, Wickham had no doubt used his time to garner the favor of their past mutual friends. It was the only way he could live as he did, by leeching off the commiseration of others.

"The Bennets would have no reason to know him, nor are they the kind of family with whom Mr. Wickham would seek to establish a friendship," continued Mrs. Reynolds. "Miss Bennet sounds promising. Miss Elizabeth, on the other hand, sounds troublesome. A lady such as she would never agree to marry for convenience if she has already refused to marry for her own comfort and security."

Mrs. Bamber nodded in agreement, saying, "Lizzy is Madeline's clear favorite, but I have to agree she would never consent to a marriage of convenience. Jane is everything lovely. Madeline's description of her is similar to how I would describe your dear departed mother, Lady Anne. Such grace and elegance."

Next, the women would conspire to convince him that marriage to Miss Bennet was a certain path to the marital bliss his father and mother had enjoyed together. Darcy cherished those memories, though he did not trust them anymore. How could his life have been so happy when every day was a struggle to hold the last shred of his family together?

He had no time for troublesome females with romantic ideals or beauties who faded like the roses at the end of summer. His heart — what was left of it — was already taken by the tiny girl sleeping against his shoulder. He smoothed a wrinkle on her gown, swearing once again, as he had hundreds of times before, to protect her.

CHAPTER 2

*E*lizabeth Bennet stood before the fireplace, her damp dress steaming. Curiosity about what would happen in the next chapter of her novel, and a shower of rain, had forced her to return to Longbourn before she had walked as far as she would have liked over the fields. Her mother and sisters had not yet returned from making calls in Meryton, meaning that Elizabeth had a few glorious, uninterrupted minutes to read in peace by the warmth of the fire.

She nestled into the nearest chair, pulling her stockinged feet up under her skirts, and opened the novel. Her finger skimmed down the page, searching for the spot where her spent candle had forced her to stop reading the night before.

Ah, yes. Lady Gwendolyn was locked in the cellar

of an abandoned castle while her evil stepfather arranged for her to marry a man in whose debt he had fallen. Isolated and without a protector, her only hope lay in Sir Knightly.

Lady Gwendolyn pulled on the chains binding her wrists, the irons biting into her flesh. Cold seeped through her torn slippers. Would Sir Knightly reach her in time?

Elizabeth's concentration was interrupted when someone stepped on a squeaky floorboard. Ancient stone castles did not squeak as Longbourn did.

Mrs. Hill greeted Elizabeth with a smile. "Your father asks for you. He is in his book room," she said.

Elizabeth sighed. Lady Gwendolyn's fate would have to hang in the balance a while longer. Closing her book with an air of resignation, Elizabeth thanked Mrs. Hill and made her way down the hall to her father's sanctuary. It was not often an invitation was extended to join him there, but Elizabeth prided herself in being the recipient of the majority of his invitations amongst her sisters. She was his favorite.

Father sipped from a wine glass, breathing with his hand over his chest as she entered the room and sat in the chair beside his desk.

"Is your cough improving, Papa?" she asked, following his gaze when he glanced at the door.

Father enjoyed the peace his book room provided from the usual noise of his household, and he had trained her well. She had closed the door behind her.

His bushy eyebrows knitted together, and he frowned.

Suspecting she knew the source of his melancholy, for they often thought so much alike, Elizabeth said, "It is much quieter without Lydia here. Sometimes I miss her, too."

Lydia, her youngest sister, had eloped with Mr. Denny, a dashing officer who had arrived in Meryton the year before with the militia. Father had disapproved of the match, but Mr. Denny had proved over the past few months to be steadier and more level-headed than his impulsive marriage to Lydia had suggested. They would never have enough money, but they loved each other. Elizabeth prayed they would be happy.

Father smiled sadly. "I wish all my girls were comfortably settled." He cleared his throat, reaching for the wine bottle when he started coughing again.

Elizabeth jumped to her feet, pouring the wine for him before he spilled it over his desk and stained the manuscripts he toiled over.

Holding the glass up to his lips, she helped him drink.

"Thank you, Lizzy," he wheezed.

"The draughts Mr. Jones prepared are not strong enough. I will write immediately to Aunt Gardiner. There must be a physician in London who has better medicine. If she cannot send it, I will collect it myself," she said, noting how pale his skin was that morning and how much deeper his cough sounded. Where his collar had fitted snuggly around his neck the month before, it now sagged.

Father held up his hand, attempting to dismiss her concerns. "Do not trouble yourself, Lizzy. I am only agitated because I have received a letter from Mr. Collins. He has a talent for putting me out of sorts."

Elizabeth dropped back into her chair. She liked Mr. Collins as much as her father did. That the clergyman had managed to marry Elizabeth's best friend, Charlotte, eight months prior (after she herself had refused him) did nothing to put the gentleman into her good graces.

"Does he write of Charlotte?" she asked.

"He implied — with the utmost delicacy, of course — that she is well despite her present condition. I remember how miserable Mrs. Bennet was toward the end of her confinement, and I suspect Mr. Collins would never admit to his wife's suffering, lest it reflect poorly on either of them. He wishes to visit us before the birth of his first child. Is that not considerate of him?" Father added sarcastically.

"All the more reason for you to get well. You must live forever and frustrate his plans of ever inheriting Longbourn," Elizabeth said cheerily.

Father did not laugh. He rubbed his hands against his face.

Elizabeth's smile suddenly felt out of place. Her imagination ran wild with explanations for his strange behavior, each one more dramatic than the last. Leaping from one conclusion to the next left her short of breath. "Papa, what is wrong?"

He took off his spectacles, laying them on top of his open book. Looking up at her with watery blue eyes, he said, "My dearest girl, I am dying."

"Nonsense!" she replied violently, her stomach sinking. "You only require different medicine. I will write to Aunt Gardiner this moment, and I will go to London myself to fetch a better draught." She rose, her need to act stronger than her desire to understand.

"Sit, Lizzy. You must listen to me."

"But you are wrong. Surely, you are wrong." He had to be wrong. People did not die of colds.

Father held her gaze, his eyes sunken and his cheeks gaunt. "Sit, Lizzy. You will listen."

"I must write to Aunt. There is no time to lose,"

she repeated, determined to make herself useful. Father only had a cold. He would be well in no time. She only needed to write to her aunt in London. The best doctors were to be found there. She turned toward the door.

"I have already written to your uncle Gardiner."

Elizabeth froze.

"There is no medicine to help me."

She reached for her chair, all the strength of purpose seeping out of her limbs.

He continued, "I wrote of my symptoms in detail, and your uncle did me the immense favor of inquiring the educated opinions of several physicians of good repute. They all agreed. I do not have a cold."

"Would it not have been better for you to go to London for a proper examination?" she asked, her voice echoing in her own head as if someone else spoke.

"Every movement brings on another fit of coughs. No, my dear. I could never make the trip."

Elizabeth shook her head. It buzzed. "We could send for a doctor to come here. Surely, if we paid enough—"

"It is no use, Lizzy. Were I an ignorant man, I might have more hope, but I read the list of symptoms. I have all of them."

The clock ticked several seconds, each one rebounding through the room more loudly than the last until the deafening noise pounded against Elizabeth's temples.

"I have consumption." With one sentence the clamor silenced.

She pressed her eyes together, her throat tight. She dropped her elbows to her knees, her forehead pressed against her palms.

Consumption. People died of consumption.

Father was beside her, pressing a teacup full of wine into her hands. "Drink, Lizzy. You must keep your strength up. You will need it. I need you to stay strong."

Powerless to do anything but obey and already missing the beloved father she would soon lose, Elizabeth took the cup and drank while he settled back in his chair. What would she do without him? All the conversations they had? The humor only he understood?

"I swore I would never use your refusal of Mr. Collins against you, and I would not mention it now were I not desperate. When I die, you, your mother and sisters..." his voice shook and his chin trembled, "...will be without a home. I have kept the true nature of my illness from your mother, and I wish for you to do the same." Taking a raspy breath, he continued, "The Gardiners have kindly offered to take Jane, but with their large family, they cannot receive Mary or Kitty."

Elizabeth squeezed her eyes shut and strained to listen. The drums in her head had calmed, but the buzz resumed.

"I have said nothing to your aunt Phillips. She is a terrible gossip and would only worry your mother before it is time. But I trust she will take Mrs. Bennet and Kitty in." Father's voice quavered, as he added, "I have not been able to secure a place for Mary ... nor for you, my dear, dear girl." He pulled his handkerchief from his pocket, rubbing it against his eyes. "Your aunt Gardiner has family in Derbyshire who might be able to help. The Bambers. Some of them are in service, and the rest are in trade, so they are only to be sought out as a last resort."

"You speak to me of status as if I care? When you tell me you are dying?"

"I will not risk ruining your prospects when your happiness is my priority."

They were words Elizabeth was grateful to hear her father pronounce, but not like this.

Father continued, "Mrs. Gardiner's assistance has been invaluable to me of late, and I know she will not rest until you and Mary are properly provided for, should I die before you have a chance to see to your own futures."

Elizabeth could bear it no longer. Pressing her cold fingers against her burning cheeks, she said, "Do not say such things, Papa. You have always recovered your health before."

"Not this time," he said, repeating with his shoulders slumped in defeat, "Not this time."

"Not if you give up so easily. You must fight!" Elizabeth insisted, her tone shrill in her ears.

She would take the evening coach to London, and she would drag a physician back to Meryton to see her father or her name was not Elizabeth Bennet. She would do what she must, but she would not let her father die if she could prevent it.

Reaching forward to clasp her hands between his own, Father said, "You must promise you will look after your mother and sisters. I am sorrier than you can ever know to charge you with this great burden, but you are clever, Lizzy. I trust you. I know you will find a way—" A violent cough interrupted his plea, and his hands tugged away from Elizabeth's in his haste to cover his mouth with the handkerchief.

That was when Elizabeth saw it. The blood.

CHAPTER 3

"*T*he letter has arrived, sir," said the butler, entering the study to hold a thick envelope resting on a salver out to Darcy.

"Thank you, Grayson," Darcy mumbled, rising from the desk and promptly forgetting the papers strewn across the surface as he cracked the seal and held the letter up to read by the light of the setting sun.

"Is there anything else you require, sir?" asked Grayson, lingering in the doorway.

Darcy looked up, irked at the interruption until he saw the concern reflected in Grayson's wrinkled brow and the hope in his attentive eyes. Like Mrs. Reynolds, Grayson had proved himself to be a reliable ally through the trials of the past year.

Relaxing his shoulders, Darcy said, "Stay, please, while I read Mr. Rochester's report. I must rely on you to keep Mrs. Reynolds informed."

Grayson bowed his head, and Darcy resumed reading.

It was not good news, but it was the news Darcy had expected unless some miracle had changed the laws since Anne's arrival into the world.

Pressing his fingers against his temples, Darcy motioned for Grayson to sit. Bad news was best heard sitting down.

Darcy skimmed through the pages again on the chance he had missed a promising detail.

He had not, unfortunately, and reading it again would do nothing to change its contents. Resisting the urge to crumple the papers and throw them into the fire, Darcy folded them and tucked the letter inside his pocket.

"Have a drink with me, Grayson," he said.

The butler did as he was bid, though Darcy noted his hesitation in drinking with his master.

Darcy had long ago ceased to measure a person's status by the norms of society. The past year had shown him who could be trusted. Honesty and loyalty were of far greater worth than one's name, fortune, or connections. In these attributes, the few servants entrusted with Anne at Pemberley were exceptional. Darcy was grateful to them for it — especially so for Anne's sake, who relied upon them entirely.

Therein lie his difficulty. Anne.

Darcy could not fail her.

He must act — and quickly.

Darcy began, "The law will not allow us to keep Anne while her father lives. Wickham's deficiencies do not signify. Unless we can convince him to sign over her guardianship, the Court of Chancery will force us to hand over the child."

At that, Grayson drank deeply. Setting down his glass, he said, "Forgive me for speaking freely, Mr. Darcy, but we cannot allow it. He would never agree to sign her care over to you when she is his means to gain a hold on Pemberley. He would use her to avenge himself against you."

Did he not know it?

Darcy leaned his elbows against his desk, the acid churning in his stomach stinging his throat. "I cannot allow him near her, and yet every day that passes increases Anne's risk of exposure. However, we must endure longer still."

Dread chilled Darcy to the bone. But there was no other option. Happiness may never be his again, but he could secure Anne.

Looking up at Grayson, Darcy voiced the maneuver he had hoped to avoid — that only desperation would move him to act upon. "I must marry as soon as it can be arranged and produce an heir of my own. Until then, Anne is not safe." He waited for the resolve of a firm decision made to fortify him, but it did not come.

"Forgive me, Mr. Darcy, please. I know you refused the idea before, but could you not consider—"

"No!" Darcy snapped. "I will not ruin Georgiana's reputation further by suggesting that the child has a father other than her husband."

"The babe's resemblance to your sister is striking. Nobody would question it after what we told Mr. Wickham..." Grayson's words trailed off.

Darcy was not a fool. Grayson's suggestion would put an end to all of their problems. But it would ruin Anne's prospects and add another lie to the growing web of deceit Darcy had been forced to build to protect her. He could not destroy her future nor would he sully Georgiana's virtue more than her elopement had already done. At least Wickham had married her. Anne had a family name. Unfortunately, it was not Darcy ... nor could it be until the courts were persuaded to allow Darcy to keep her — an impossibility according to Mr. Rochester and every other knowledgeable solicitor, barrister, and judge well-versed in the laws of guardianship and adoption at Chancery.

Grabbing a piece of paper, Darcy said, "Wickham is greedy and selfish. He will only be interested in Anne for what he can gain through her. If she no longer stands to inherit Pemberley, then she will no longer be of any use to him. She will be safe." He scribbled a hasty note. He would have to act faster than his emotions allowed or he would never be able to do what he must. Once the ink dried, Darcy folded the paper and wrote Bingley's name on it. "See this is delivered to Bingley immediately. I will leave for Hertfordshire as soon as the preparations are made."

"Hertfordshire?" Grayson's eyes widened, and he downed the last of the amber liquid in his glass in one gulp.

"Wickham is too well-known in Derbyshire. I cannot risk marrying a lady who might sympathize with him. I must attempt to unite myself with a lady who will prove loyal to a child not her own — a lady recommended to me by the persons I trust most."

What Darcy sought was impossible, but he had to try. The eldest Bennet daughter was his most promising solution, and so he would begin his daunting search in Hertfordshire.

He would do anything for Anne. Even forsake his own love and happiness to marry for convenience.

CHAPTER 4

ONE WEEK LATER

arcy rubbed his eyes and drained his cup. The coffee was bitter and strong, and Darcy prayed it would serve its purpose. He needed his senses about him.

"The carriage is ready," Bingley said, clapping his hands together. He had talked of nothing but the Meryton Assembly all day.

Darcy wished he could share in his friend's excitement. He would rather have retired early. He had only arrived at Netherfield Park the day before. What Darcy had intended to be an easy journey had been complicated by Mrs. Reynolds when she insisted he travel in style — as befits a gentleman seeking to woo a lady.

The housekeeper, no doubt motivated by warm memories of Darcy's own parents, still hoped for a romance. Theirs had been love at first sight.

Darcy was too practical for that. There was not time for love. By necessity, his would be a marriage of convenience — a small sacrifice when Anne's security lay in the balance.

While he was practical, Darcy was not cruel. He allowed Mrs. Reynolds and his valet to pack more clothes than he could ever wear in the time it took him to complete negotiations with the father of the lady he would choose. (He had, however, drawn the line in their interference when they suggested he stop in London for a new wardrobe. He was not a dandy, nor did he wish to wed a woman who fancied his waistcoat more than his character.) His aim was simple. A marriage of convenience with a trust-worthy lady who would be content with the security and comfort he could purchase for her. There were few who required more, and he expected nothing less. He had brought his mother's wedding ring.

Darcy followed Bingley out to the carriage where Mr. Hurst endured the cutting remarks of his wife and her younger sister, Miss Bingley. There was a lady who would have jumped at the opportunity to elevate herself in society by marrying Darcy. But she did not like children and was too often inconsiderate of anyone's needs and wishes but her own. Miss Bingley would make a contentious wife, and Darcy had enough conflict to manage without adding her to it. It was the same reasoning which kept Darcy from Kent and his aunt Catherine, who insisted he marry his cousin, Anne. (The name did not suit her at all, whereas it had his mother and Georgiana's child, and he resented Aunt Catherine's presumption in granting it to her weakling daughter.)

The future Mrs. Darcy must be kind, discreet, and trustworthy. She must be capable of some affection if she would make a suitable mother for Anne … and their eventual heir. Darcy cleared his throat and shifted his weight on the carriage squabs. *This is for Anne. Anything for Anne. A sensible lady would be honored to receive the offer I am willing to give,* he reminded himself once again.

"You are uncommonly quiet this evening, Mr. Darcy," said Miss Bingley.

Her coy smile was wasted on him. Darcy looked out of the carriage window. The moon illuminated the roads and glowed over the fields, filling him with such a longing to return to Pemberley — how it had once been — that his throat did not permit him to utter an immediate reply.

Would Anne sleep without him there to rock her? Every day away from her was torture. Mrs. Reynolds was true to her promise to write daily, but it was not the same. Unable to check on Anne at night, to see her peaceful form slumbering in her crib, Darcy's sleep had been restless at best. He would not be able to rest until he returned and saw with his own eyes that she was well.

"I do not blame you for dreading the evening ahead of us. We cannot expect to find any society worth having at this rustic event, but Charles insists we should mix company with these countrified villagers and peasants," Miss Bingley added with a haughty snort.

Bingley discouraged her snobbery, saying, "If you cannot think of something pleasant to say, I beg you to keep your cutting remarks to yourself, Caroline. That goes for you, too, Louisa. You both know it was our father's wish for me to buy an estate and settle like a gentleman. Whom do you think we would depend upon to maintain a proper living but the very peasants you scorn?"

Darcy nodded at Bingley. The year before, his friend would have ignored his sister's arrogant speech. Not anymore. Not when he had been the master of his own choices and had been forced to deal with the consequences of his father's outdated mills long enough to benefit from them. Responsibility had settled well on Bingley.

Miss Bingley huffed, but she said nothing the rest of the drive to Meryton. The trip was more pleasant for her silence.

The door opened, and Darcy alighted with Bingley to assist the ladies. The moment he had dreaded had finally arrived, and it only remained for him to summon his courage and press forward to his goal.

Bingley observed his surroundings aloud with great pleasure, commenting on the number of people present and the size of the assembly room once they entered. Having nothing pleasant to say, his sisters refrained from commenting at all. Mr. Hurst, only interested in cards and his next meal, went directly to the refreshment table to fetch his first glass of punch, rudely leaving Darcy and Bingley alone with the ladies to face the crowded hall.

The music paused. Conversations faded. Every eye turned their way.

Darcy felt like a display at an exposition. A cold sweat broke over him. His fingers turned into icicles.

Remembering his purpose, he forced a smile.

When it felt more like a grimace, Darcy bowed to disguise his discomfort. The sooner he met the eldest Bennet daughter, the better.

An older gentleman stepped through the crowd to approach them, his grand gestures and welcoming manner easily identifying him as the Master of Ceremonies. Sir William Lucas was his name, but Darcy did not trouble himself to remember it. Bennet was the only name of interest to him that evening.

Georgiana would have teased Darcy endlessly for his nervousness. That she was not there to do so tore at his chest. The cheerful music that resumed along with trills of laughter and conversation added to Darcy's bleakness. How could they carry on and enjoy themselves when they would never know Georgiana's laughter? When Little Anne would never know her mother?

Anne. He was there for Anne. Darcy stood taller and straightened his waistcoat.

While he held none of Mrs. Reynolds' romantic illusions (marriages of convenience allowed little room for love), Darcy had sense enough to know that no woman would wish to hold second candle to the sister still foremost in his thoughts. He had removed the black ribbons around his coat sleeve and hat, replacing them with a smaller token of his remembrance — a black opal pierced through his cravat. The bright, iridescent colors made the dark parts of the stone bleaker. God, he missed her. He missed Anne. She would be bigger when he returned to Pemberley.

Faces turned to him, and Darcy startled to attention. They seemed to expect a reply from him.

If only he knew what had been asked.

With a warm smile, Bingley said, "You must forgive Darcy, Sir William. It is a wonder he accompanied us at all this evening when he only arrived from Derbyshire yesterday."

Bless Bingley. He was a good friend.

"From Derbyshire, you say? That is quite a journey, and we are honored Mr. Darcy has joined us when most gentlemen would rather rest. It is a testament to your character that you overlook your own comfort to appear at our humble assembly, Mr. Darcy," Sir William said with a grand bow.

Grateful to Bingley for smoothing over his gaffe and to Sir William for generously accepting it, Darcy smiled in earnest, determined not to make any more blunders while he was being so closely observed. "Thank you for your welcome and understanding, Sir William."

The older gentleman grinned at him. "It will be my honor to help you make introductions. The

Bennets — their estate is in nearby Longbourn — have family in Derbyshire, if I am not mistaken." He turned, rising as tall as his stretched neck allowed.

He did not have to search long. Shoving her way through the crowd was a matron who pulled four young ladies behind her. The intensity of her fixed gaze made Darcy feel like a target to her determined arrow. Under normal circumstances, he would have excused himself.

But there was nothing normal about what he planned to do, nor did he wish to delay the inevitable further. The woman barging a path through the assembly too accurately matched Mrs. Bamber's horrific description of Mrs. Bennet for him to turn away.

Widening his stance, Darcy rooted his feet in place and prepared himself to meet the mother of the lady who might become his bride.

"Ah, there is Mrs. Bennet," said Sir William.

He introduced the family with great alacrity, but Darcy did not need to hear their names pronounced to know wherein his interest lie.

The eldest, Miss Jane Bennet, was as lovely and fair as Mrs. Bamber had claimed her to be. She blushed and bowed her head charmingly. Her voice was gentle when Bingley complimented her. Darcy understood Mrs. Bamber's comparison to his own mother. Miss Bennet was the picture of grace and elegance.

Darcy relaxed. If she replied favorably to the series of questions he had prepared, she would do.

Miss Elizabeth, however, looked Darcy straight in the eye. Her directness would have been disturbing were it not for the upward curve of her lips and the glint in her eyes. He sensed she saw a great deal more than he was comfortable with, but there was nothing malicious in her aspect to give rise to concern.

Darcy could not help but wonder what she observed.

CHAPTER 5

*M*r. Darcy was the very personification of Sir Knightly. Tall, dark, handsome, and with a hint of mystery about him. Elizabeth was intrigued, but her attention was pulled away from him, drawn to his fair friend who could not keep silent in his admiration for Jane. If love were a lightning bolt, then it had struck the moment Sir William introduced Mr. Bingley to Jane. Anyone could see he was pleased with her, and Jane would not disappoint him when he came to know her character. Jane was just as she appeared to be: gentle, kind, attentive … and everything else a gentleman would appreciate in a wife.

There was hope! If Mr. Bingley married Jane, and if he was as kind as first impressions implied him to be, then their futures were as good as secured.

Elizabeth reined her thoughts in before caprice carried them away. They had only just been introduced, and already she was planning the wedding! She was becoming as bad as her mother, who was doing everything in her power to secure dances for her daughters before Sir William had a chance to introduce the new arrivals to the other ladies present at the assembly.

Taking Mama's blatant hints in good humor, Mr. Bingley asked Jane for a dance.

So pleased was Elizabeth with her sister's immediate success, she had to stifle a gasp when Mr. Darcy said her name.

"Miss Elizabeth, might I have the pleasure of your company for this dance?" he asked, his voice deep and smooth like melted butter.

"I would be delighted, Mr. Darcy," she said, earning claps from her mother and scowls from the rest of the gentlemen's party. Elizabeth cared not. She loved to dance, and her partner was unquestionably the handsomest gentleman in the room. That he sounded exactly how she imagined Sir Knightly to sound was an extra delight. If Mr. Darcy danced as gracefully as he had entered the ballroom, then the next quarter of an hour would be enough to carry Elizabeth through the rest of the evening — wherein her toes were certain to be trodden upon by several well-meaning, but clumsy, partners.

She and Mr. Darcy took their places next to Mr. Bingley and Jane, who were so enraptured with each other, they did not seem to notice anyone or anything aside from themselves.

Optimism added a bounce to Elizabeth's steps and a smile she could not temper to her face. Their futures were not so bleak as her father feared. Not so long as the medicine she had sent for helped him. Three bottles had arrived two days before, and it seemed to be helping.

And Mr. Bingley was dancing with Jane.

What a joyous night it was turning out to be!

Turning her attention to her own partner, Elizabeth caught Mr. Darcy scowling at nothing in particular. When he caught her eye, he forced a smile.

Interesting.

He said a touch too jovially, "Sir William mentioned you have family in Derbyshire. I wonder if you are related to the Bambers?"

Elizabeth stifled a gasp. Why should a highborn gentleman know them when they were either in trade or service? The man was an intriguing contrast. On one hand, he exerted himself to smile and show an interest in conversation. On the other hand, Elizabeth could not shake the sensation that Mr. Darcy would rather be anywhere but at the assembly.

A turn in the dance afforded her the opportunity to examine him before she replied. How strange he should wear a black opal in his cravat. Most gentlemen of means flaunted their fortunes with flashy diamonds or bright gems. In comparison, a black opal was easy to overlook. It was somber — much too somber for an assembly. Perhaps Mr. Darcy was shy and did not wish to draw attention to himself.

Their palms touched, and the reply on the tip of Elizabeth's tongue vanished. Gone. She looked at their joined hands, a warm sizzle washing over her as if she had partaken of too much punch when she had yet to drink even one glass. What was this dizzying deliciousness?

It was not until they reached the end of the promenade and Mr. Darcy's hand left Elizabeth's that she would recover her thoughts.

Fighting the blush heating her neck and cheeks, she said, "My aunt's family lives in Derbyshire. Is Lambton near Pemberley?"

Mr. Darcy did not seem to notice her breathy tone or overheated face. If he did, he was too much of a gentleman to tease her. He answered coolly, "It is. Mrs. Bamber is a trustworthy woman, and she speaks highly of—" he looked about as if he had lost his words, his cheeks taking on a hint of red.

His awkwardness put Elizabeth at ease in an instant. This was a gentleman for whom conversation did not come easily, at least, not with new acquaintances. Yes, Mr. Darcy must be dreadfully shy, she concluded.

She helped him on. There could only be one lady of their mutual acquaintance of whom her Lambton relatives would speak so highly. "Of Mrs. Madeline Gardiner? She is my aunt. Mrs. Bamber has every reason to praise her. My aunt is sensible, kind, and good. She is the sort of friend with whom one may speak freely without misunderstandings or breaches of confidence. Family is important to her, so she writes and visits often."

He exhaled, and Elizabeth supposed he must be very nervous indeed.

"You have not visited the Peak District?" he asked.

Elizabeth had never suffered shyness, but she knew from her own sister that the timid only required some drawing out to encourage conversation and put them at ease. Appreciating Mr. Darcy's attempts to be good company, Elizabeth reciprocated with a smile and an inviting reply. "I have not yet, though it has been a desire of mine to go. So little of England outside of Hertfordshire and parts of London are known to me, and I should like very much to explore the country more. Pray, tell me about Derbyshire, Mr. Darcy. Perhaps I shall finally tour the area and meet my aunt's family next summer."

His eyes warmed, and Elizabeth wished she had noticed for a certainty what color they were when they had first been introduced. Right now, they were a greenish gold where she would have sworn his eyes were an amber hue the minute before.

"Of course, I am partial to Pemberley and the villages surrounding it. The fields blossom with lavender. Wind-bent trees house all manner of birds…" A far-off look took Mr. Darcy away from Elizabeth long before the steps of the dance separated them.

He was homesick, poor man. What on earth had brought him to Hertfordshire?

She decided Mr. Darcy was a gentleman worth knowing, shy as he was. His manners were awkward, but his effort to be amiable earned her sympathy. Plus, he liked lavender enough to make mention of it, and she had always favored the scent. Elizabeth wondered if he could smell it on her hair. But, of course, that was ridiculous. They were not standing near enough, and there were too many bodies overpowering the delicate scent for him to notice.

He remained quiet when, once again, they returned to each other's side. He fingered the black gemstone, not once losing step to the tune.

"You miss Pemberley," she stated.

"Yes."

When he said nothing more, Elizabeth attempted to turn the topic to one which always made her happy. Books. "I hope Mr. Bingley's library offers a comforting sanctuary wherein you might find respite. Books make constant friends, loyally telling the same story and filling one with the same delight they generously gave on the first reading."

Now his eyes were decidedly green around the pupils. "I agree with your comparison of books to loyal friends, but I have never been tempted to read the same story more than once."

Elizabeth gasped. "You do not know what you miss, sir." She had finished reading Lady Gwendolyn and Sir Knightly's romantic adventure, and already she looked forward to reading it again.

Mr. Darcy's comment added further insight into his character. He was not so similar to Jane as Elizabeth had supposed. Jane would never disagree with anyone, much less with a new acquaintance, and

Elizabeth found that she was pleased with Mr. Darcy's contrary opinion.

The incredulous arch of his thick eyebrow as well as her own pleasure in a good debate encouraged Elizabeth to continue. "Have you never wished to renew an old acquaintance? I am always pleasantly surprised at the insights time and distance add to a friendship … or, in this case, a book."

One corner of his lips curled upward. "Is not the greatest thrill in reading a novel — I presume you refer to novels for entertainment, as I have found educational tomes to be neither inviting nor friendly…"

Elizabeth giggled. "You assume correctly, although I would not exclude educational works meant to expand the mind and increase one's understanding entirely. I will own, however, that I have not been tempted to read any such books more than once."

Mr. Darcy had a pleasant smile. It spread over his face, crinkling the corners of his eyes and exposing white teeth. "Very well," he said, "Far be it from me to discourage the improvement of one's mind through extensive reading. However, returning to my original argument, do you not feel that the greatest thrill to come from a book is the surprise and satisfaction felt when the characters meet their just endings, be they tragic or happy?"

She shook her head enthusiastically. "The world is full enough of suffering for me to choose to read more misery. I would rather laugh than cry. Give me a happy ending over a heart-wrenching tragedy any day, and I will savor my second reading in eager expectation of sharing in their joy once again, knowing how well they deserve such happiness."

His smile widened, then faded. "You speak of the characters as if they were real. Would that everyone could be happy," he said softly.

Once more, the steps of the dance separated them, and when they met again, Mr. Darcy's smile was in place. It did not, however, reach his eyes.

Elizabeth did not know what to make of him.

His manners were notably more guarded when he said, "When we have public assemblies in the village near my estate, there are always children about. I do not see many here. Are they discouraged from attending?"

What a strange observation. Elizabeth looked about the room, seeing the usual mix of age and society present. Shrugging her shoulders, she said, "My mother has always encouraged my sisters and me to accompany her — no matter what our ages were — so we might visit our neighbors, make new acquaintances, and dance. The country does not offer much more by way of entertainment, and we are accustomed to seizing what diversion we can. I would think other families are similar, though I do not presume to speak for them."

More directly, he asked, "Do you like children?"

Inwardly applauding Mr. Darcy's growing boldness, Elizabeth answered in kind. "I adore children. My sister, Jane, has a way with babes which I envy, but my favorite age is when a child is old enough to begin exploring the world; when their curiosity widens their eyes with wonder and they ask all manner of outrageous questions."

He seemed pleased with her answer, though she could only imagine why (and already, her imagination was hard at work making sense of his strange and not entirely appropriate question.)

Elizabeth was beginning to doubt her initial impression of Mr. Darcy. He was not shy.

Their dance ended, and he offered to see her to the refreshment table. It was hot in the room, and her curiosity regarding the gentleman had yet to be satisfied. If anything, she wished to know more about him.

She sipped slowly from the glass he handed to her. "Thank you, Mr. Darcy, for the dance and the punch."

He looked positively miserable. Not the reaction she had meant to inspire.

Mr. Darcy was too new an acquaintance to press, and so she sipped from her glass and swayed to the music.

"Must love always be part of the happy ending? Can not a union made for an honorable purpose be happy without it?" he asked, once again startling her. His intense gaze bored into Elizabeth as if she were the only person in the room.

Definitely not shy.

Not having the luxury of anticipating the sudden turn of conversation, Elizabeth replied a touch too boldly. "Is it not our purpose to love and be loved? Otherwise, why should we bother to live at all? I am convinced love is the key to happiness."

"You would not be content to marry for convenience or security? Most ladies are."

"I am not accustomed to being swayed by the values of others. On the contrary, I am convinced that nothing but the most intense love will persuade me to marry." She held his eyes with hers, unwilling to look away before he did, lest he doubt her. She held no hope of ever seeing Mr. Darcy again after that pretty admission. Loving wives expected much of the men they married — honesty, selfless consideration, regard for their opinions, to be cherished, valued… *And rightly so if they were the ones to endure childbirth,* thought Elizabeth rebelliously, still holding his gaze.

"Do your sisters share your view?" he asked.

"Ask them if you dare. I cannot speak for them." She was smart enough to keep her thoughts to herself when she had already said too much. Most gentlemen would run in the opposite direction.

Mr. Darcy walked.

CHAPTER 6

arcy liked Miss Elizabeth. Her positive outlook and lighthearted manners had made him forget himself, forget his troubles. Therein lay her danger. He had not meant to ask such a bold question, but the spark in her brown eyes had challenged him. Her answer had been immediate and definite, closing a door firmly in his face. She believed a marriage should be born from a deep love, as he did. She would never agree to a union unless it met with her requirements, and Darcy did not have the time to offer what she desired. It was a pity. Under more favorable circumstances, he would have tried.

Darcy walked around the room, renewing his resolve. He would dance with Miss Jane Bennet next.

A hearty laugh drew his attention over to a group

gathered around the refreshment table. Miss Elizabeth smiled and conversed easily with her neighbors. He ought to have known she was the source of the gaiety.

Farther down the length of the room, in a smaller group, Miss Bennet patiently listened while Bingley expounded passionately on his chosen subject. To be fair, Bingley rarely spoke of anything without a good deal of animation.

Darcy made his way over to them.

Though she clearly enjoyed her present company, Miss Bennet was too polite to refuse Darcy's request for a dance. A lady such as she would never speak out of turn, but he would be hard-pressed to hear her true opinion … if she had one. How unlike Miss Elizabeth, who had boldly pronounced her views, though they ran contrary to his needs.

Miss Bennet was a graceful partner and lovely to look upon, but Darcy's frustration mounted when he was unable to delicately extract the information he required before he could make an offer. Not for fear of offense (Miss Bennet was much too complacent to be easily offended), but for the realization that her agreeable manners would make it difficult for her to refuse *any* offer made to her. Even an offer of marriage from a man she had only recently met.

Where he ought to be gratified (Was this not

what he sought?), Darcy was overcome with misgivings he tried to ignore.

Had not Miss Elizabeth said that Miss Bennet was good with children? She would be kind and gentle with Anne. What was more, Darcy's sudden union with such a lady would not be questioned. Society would assume her pale beauty had captured his heart as his mother had captured his father's.

He bowed over Miss Bennet's hand at the end of the dance, allowing her to be swept away by the next gentleman waiting for his chance to work his charm on the lady.

Darcy tried to recall their conversation, for he had not remained silent. He supposed she had given some reply, but for the life of him, he could not remember a word.

Her company was tepid compared to Miss Elizabeth, but at least Miss Bennet would be agreeable. He would provide her a handsome allowance and the most beautiful estate in which to reside. He would treat her with consideration, proving loyal and honorable in all his actions. Few ladies wished for more than that. Few were like Miss Elizabeth. Thank goodness for that.

Sir William performed his duties grandly, taking it upon himself to introduce Darcy to every lady present over the course of the evening — eligible or otherwise.

Several times, Darcy found his sight wandering about the room to find Miss Elizabeth. Merely out of curiosity, of course. The closer he observed the family, the more certain he could be about their characters.

She laughed, danced, and conversed, leaving a wake of joyous friends and lively discussions behind her while Miss Bennet's subdued conversation, graceful dancing, and cool manners would have made her the belle of a society ball.

The Bennets were everything Mrs. Bamber had claimed they would be, and by the time Bingley had danced his fill and Darcy's feet throbbed, he had decided on his course. He would call on Mr. Bennet at Longbourn on the morrow.

Darcy would marry Miss Bennet by the end of the week.

"Is Miss Jane Bennet not an angel, Darcy? I admit I have never been so taken with a lady as I was with her this evening." Bingley swirled the brandy in his glass and propped one booted foot on top of his knee.

Darcy dropped into his chair, feeling as if the rug had been pulled out from under his feet.

Of all the ladies present, why did Bingley have to settle on Miss Bennet? On *his* choice?

While Darcy formulated a comment meant to discourage his friend, Bingley discoursed on Miss Bennet's attributes — all of which were exceedingly fine according to him. That most of her praise was based on her character rather than her appearance did credit to his friend, and Darcy soon found himself in a quandary.

He could not make an offer no father would refuse when his own dear friend showed a marked preference for the lady. Just because he doubted he could ever be happy did not mean he wished to deny Bingley the opportunity of making a blissful union.

However, Bingley was infamously fickle. While he had matured in many other areas of his life, it remained to be seen if his heart had become as steady as his mind.

"Do you mean to court her, then?" Darcy asked, holding his breath.

Bingley colored. "You do not think it too forward of me? Too rushed?"

Before Mr. Rochester's letter, Darcy would have encouraged Bingley to be patient, to think and act slowly. But who was he to criticize a hasty courtship when he himself intended to skip right to marriage? He said, "I am not qualified to offer my opinion, as I am unmarried."

"Come, Darcy. You know me better than anyone — better than myself oftentimes. I appeal to you as a friend. Am I ready? Have I matured enough to take responsibility not only for my own happiness, but for that of another?"

Drat. Exhaling with a sigh, Darcy said, "That you concern yourself with your future wife's happiness as well as your own bodes well for both of you, but I will refrain from saying anything else. You are not as impulsive as you used to be, and I praise you for it. However, there comes a time when you must learn to trust your own instincts."

Darcy held on to the diminishing possibility that Bingley would back off and he could continue with his plan.

Bingley rubbed his fingers over his chin. "Thank you, Darcy. The troubles at my father's mill over the past year forced me neither to take important decisions lightly nor to ignore the effect my choices have on others. But marriage is the greatest decision, is it not? I wish to choose wisely and avoid a lifetime of regret."

Darcy's prospects looked bleaker. He asked, "Do

you believe you would regret a life with Miss Bennet?"

This was the moment of truth.

Bingley's shoulders slumped. "I cannot know for a certainty. It is too soon."

Darcy was too elated to pity Bingley.

"But I am willing to risk my heart to find out." Sitting forward abruptly and shoving his fist into the air, Bingley startled Darcy further when he added, "I am, and I will. Tomorrow, I will return Mr. Bennet's call at Longbourn. He was the first gentleman to welcome me to Hertfordshire, and it would only be proper for me to pay him a call. Will you come with me?"

Drat it all.

There was nothing else to be done. Darcy would have to alter his plan.

He would go to Longbourn on the morrow, but he would not go to propose.

CHAPTER 7

*E*lizabeth tried to enjoy the silence at Longbourn, but the pattering rain and crackling fire did not grant her the solace they normally bestowed. Nor could Lady Gwendolyn's troubles enrapture her as they had at her first reading.

"With the manner you keep sighing, one might think you were crossed in love," Father said, peeking briefly at her from the top of his book before returning his attention to the page.

Turning away from the window facing the drive to the warmth of the fire, Elizabeth heard the sound she had dreaded hearing all day — the crunch of carriage wheels on their drive.

"That will be Mr. Collins," she grumbled, already dreading his visit. Mr. Collins had the unique ability to suck the joy out of any occasion. "It does not bode well for Charlotte that her husband prefers to spend the final weeks of her confinement securing his inheritance here rather than tending to her at Hunsford."

Her odious cousin had not crossed Longbourn's threshold yet, and already Elizabeth was in a black study. She ought to have accompanied her mother and sisters into Meryton. They had been wise to make calls rather than wait around, as she had, for the clergyman who would eventually cast them from the only home they had ever known. How she loathed him.

Father looked up again, his mouth open to reply until his vision fixed on the window. "That does not look like Mr. Collins," he said, surprising Elizabeth when he tidied the scattered papers on the table beside his chair into a neat pile. He never tidied anything, preferring his own system of what he called "organized chaos" wherein he could locate any item in a pile an uninformed observer would declare to be a hopeless mess.

She turned to see what had inspired his uncharacteristic orderliness, but whoever was outside had already passed by the window. The view was too blurry to see much anyway. Who else but Mr. Collins would travel in this weather? (Besides her own mother and sisters ... who had only ventured out of doors in order to avoid the nuisance.) No, it must be Mr. Collins.

Father rose from his chair. His color was better than it had been the day before, and though Elizabeth had been listening for it, she had not heard the wheezing breath that preceded a coughing fit. The new draught was working. As hopeful as she was, Elizabeth prayed Mr. Collins would not witness any coughing episodes. He would delight in them, moving himself and his family into Longbourn in eager expectation of Father's early demise under the pretense of offering his comfort and assistance. Then, they would never be rid of the clergyman.

Mr. Hill appeared in the doorway, but it was not Mr. Collins he announced.

"Mr. Darcy and Mr. Bingley are here to see you, sir," he said.

Elizabeth snapped upright, wishing she had imitated her father and tidied a bit. As it was, she only had time enough to grab Kitty's wad of tangled ribbons and stuff them under a cushion. She would not allow for her younger sister's slovenly habits to cause Mr. Bingley to doubt Jane's ability to manage a household. Nor did she wish for Mr. Darcy to believe her sloppy ... if he thought about her at all.

"Send them in, Hill," Father replied eagerly.

Elizabeth did not have a chance to ask if he had been expecting the gentlemen callers, and he only confounded her further when he winked at her just as Mr. Darcy and Mr. Bingley stepped into the drawing room.

Mr. Darcy smiled. By all appearances, he was pleased to see her when Elizabeth had been certain he would go out of his way to avoid her. Had he not ignored her for the rest of the Meryton Assembly? To his credit, he had danced with every female in the room. But he had not sought her company again, though there had been many opportunities when he might have done so, had he wished it.

Elizabeth had been a little disappointed he had chosen to keep his distance. Mr. Darcy was nothing to her, but he was interesting. She would not have minded a few minutes more of his conversation.

Bows and greetings were exchanged, and Father rang for tea while apologizing for the absence of Mrs. Bennet and his other daughters.

Mr. Bingley disguised his disappointment well, but Elizabeth had been looking for signs of it. She saw the brief dimming of his countenance before his overenthusiastic attempt to cover it over.

On the other hand, Mr. Darcy seemed relieved. His countenance was pleasant and relaxed as he smiled at Father before taking a seat opposite him.

He had a pleasant smile. It softened his eyes. Beds of moss on damp earth. Or damp earth spotted with moss? Elizabeth could not decide which, but discreetly looked away before she was caught staring.

"How are you enjoying Hertfordshire?" Father asked, nestling against his chair and crossing one leg over the other, completely at ease.

"I am enjoying it very much," Mr. Bingley replied. "Our neighbors are hospitable and have made us feel most welcome."

Father grinned. Mother had ensured he was one of the first to call upon Mr. Bingley at Netherfield Park. "And you, Mr. Darcy? I daresay we do not have the culture and society to which you are accustomed, but what we lack in variety, we make up for in sincerity."

"I would not trade sincerity for society," Mr. Darcy replied, his voice deep and firm.

"Would you not?" Father said, pinching his chin as he always did when his mind was engaged. There were few things he enjoyed more than a philosophical debate.

Mr. Darcy said, "I have no use for people who hide what they are behind their surname and status."

Elizabeth looked at him askance. That was a bold statement from one born into the highest circles.

Father was intrigued. Truth be told, Elizabeth was too.

"Would you choose to befriend a trustworthy laborer rather than a peer known to merely distort the truth to his or her advantage without any intent to harm?" she asked.

Mr. Darcy's golden green eyes fixed on her, and Elizabeth felt her neck warm.

"A person's character is dependent on his or her values. These are made evident by one's actions. I care not to befriend those lacking the qualities I esteem, nor would I deny myself the pleasure of association with one who does. That said, I do not make friends easily."

Father sat forward in his chair, his hands clasped together. "I suppose you make a study of character then before you extend your friendship to anyone?"

"Of course," Mr. Darcy said, shifting his gaze over to Father.

"How extraordinary! It fascinates me to observe how easily the multitudes are swayed by superficial charm. I wonder how you are able to avoid being swayed by popular opinion through your analysis..."

If Father slid forward another inch in his chair, he was in danger of falling to the floor. It was, however, good to see him fully engaged in worthwhile conversation.

Mr. Darcy did not disappoint. "I am not easily swayed by anything when my mind is made up."

"A difficult accomplishment indeed when emotions get involved, as they often do," observed Father.

"Not when one makes a habit of thinking rationally. Like all thoughts, we may choose how and what we think. We are not slaves to them or our emotions."

This cold speech did not reflect Elizabeth's impression of the man himself. She had studied the stoic beliefs on detached emotion in the diaries of Marcus Aurelius, and while she agreed that one should not allow herself to be governed by emotions, she did not wish to completely part with them. She wondered how intensely Mr. Darcy adhered to the stoic philosophy.

Father was delighted. "While I do my best to keep an open mind, I own I see many advantages to a decisive, narrowed mind. I do not accuse you of close-mindedness, Mr. Darcy, for your very answers imply a great deal of study and thought, but I refer to the characteristics of focus and intent. I may surmise, then, that it is a true compliment to those to whom you have extended your friendship." He smiled at Mr. Bingley.

Mr. Bingley straightened his spine, his cheeks

reflecting a merry countenance. "I had never considered how Darcy's approval reflected favorably on me, but I see the compliment now and am honored. I have a reputation for getting on with everyone I meet, but in matters of import there are very few in whom I would confide. Darcy is one of the few, as he is with many others who rely on his guidance."

While they would shower Mr. Darcy with praise, to which he neither reacted with a puffed up chest nor with embarrassment, Elizabeth could not help but find some flaws in Mr. Bingley's reasoning. Her forehead furrowed, and had her mother been there, she would have scolded Elizabeth for the creases in her skin.

Father noticed. With a knowing chuckle, he said, "Ah, there it is. Your observation has intrigued my Lizzy, Mr. Bingley. Like Mr. Darcy, she delights in sketching the characters of the people she meets. I wonder, what has piqued your curiosity, my girl?"

Elizabeth desired an answer, but not at the expense of asking her question. It was too intimate.

Seeking more agreeable ground, she replied, "Mr. Darcy is too new an acquaintance to suffer the consequences of my curiosity. He may choose to reveal what he wishes, and I will draw the conclusions to which his actions lead."

Mr. Darcy met her eyes again, and she could not

look away from the challenge she saw in their verdant gold depths.

How could she ever have thought he was shy?

His eyebrow raised, and there was a touch of humor in his tone when he said, "I should like to hear your thoughts, Miss Elizabeth, if you wish to share them."

It was a dare to which Elizabeth could not fail to respond. "I find your character a study of contrasts. On first acquaintance, I would have described you as shy and awkward in conversation. As if you have been denied society for a long time. There were moments I sensed your melancholy, though you attempted to hide it."

She ignored Mr. Bingley's gasp, continuing, "However, your discussion today paints the picture of a self-assured, decisive gentleman who does not fear the scorn of society if it means compromising his values. Such an honorable person would see his duty in making himself agreeable in society, whether he wished for their approval or not."

Mr. Bingley clapped. Addressing Father, he said, "She is good. That describes Darcy perfectly."

But Elizabeth was not done. Mr. Darcy watched her unwaveringly, and the firm constancy of his look emboldened her to add, "I do have to wonder ... where does an individual, whose opinion is always sought after and highly regarded, turn for support when he requires assistance? Where does he find relief for his burdens? Or must he always bear them alone?"

Elizabeth saw the shift in Mr. Darcy's eyes, but she did not know what it meant. The muscles at his jaw twitched. Had she been overly bold or had she struck too close to the truth? Perhaps the gentleman was not as unaffected as he had claimed.

She would have apologized and changed the subject, but he had asked for her observation ... and the tea arrived. By the time she poured, Mr. Darcy had recovered himself so well, Elizabeth began to doubt what she had seen. She hardly knew the man. Who was she to suppose she had any effect on him at all? He had asked for her opinion, and she had told him. As for her question ... he probably thought it impertinent and would forget it and her as soon as he and Mr. Bingley departed from Longbourn.

The conversation took a much lighter turn when Mr. Bingley inquired after the other ladies of the house.

"Had they known you would call, they would have been present. But I fear they will miss you in their endeavor to avoid the arrival of another gentleman whom I am certain Mr. Darcy would never befriend. Such haughty displays of humility and studied compliments you cannot have previously witnessed. If he stays as long as he threatens, I daresay you shall have to meet him. I only hope I am present for the occasion," Father said with a chuckle.

Which turned into a wheeze.

Which turned into a cough.

Which turned into a full out attack on Father's lungs as he struggled for air.

CHAPTER 8

*D*arcy lunged forward before Mr. Bennet toppled to the floor. Miss Elizabeth whisked around to her father's other side, cushioning his head as Darcy carefully lowered him to the carpet.

Reaching over to the table, Miss Elizabeth grabbed Mr. Bennet's teacup, holding it to his lips. Tea dribbled over her fingers and soaked into her gown, but she held the cup as steadily as she could while she fumbled with his cravat with the other. Her quick thinking was impressive. Another lady would have swooned.

"Allow me," Darcy said, making quick work of loosening the fabric, which the older gentleman pressed against his mouth like a handkerchief.

Bingley appeared in the doorway with the housekeeper. She held out a bottle with an inch of liquid at the bottom to Miss Elizabeth.

Taking the bottle, Miss Elizabeth lifted it to his lips, saying softly, "Drink, Papa. There are two more bottles in the top drawer of Father's desk. Will you please fetch one, Mrs. Hill?" she asked.

The housekeeper stepped forward, her hands clutched together. "That was where I got that bottle, Miss. There are no more."

Miss Elizabeth inhaled sharply.

Mr. Bennet's cough subsided, though he breathed with difficulty. His chest rattled like a child slurping his soup. He wadded the makeshift handkerchief in his hand, lowering it to his chest.

Bingley stepped forward. "Is the draught from the apothecary?" he asked.

"No, but he must have something. We will have to send for Mr. Jones in Meryton," Miss Elizabeth said.

Mrs. Hill nodded.

Miss Elizabeth's ability to make wise decisions under duress, as well as her swiftness in communicating clearly so that an order could be carried out, impressed Darcy. His instincts about her at the ball had not been wrong.

"I will go to Meryton and fetch more immediately," Bingley said, holding up his hands to ward off

Miss Elizabeth's protest. "Please. It would be a kindness for you to allow me to help. I cannot look on when I can *do* something. My horse is ready and fast. Let me go."

"Thank you, Mr. Bingley. Mr. Jones is often found at the room above the haberdashery," she said. She sounded so weary. While her eyes were as fine and full of life as Darcy remembered them being at their first meeting, he now noticed the dark rims circling them. Her smile was quick and ready, but he now saw the effort with which she forced her lips upward. Her shoulders were stiff. Her chin lifted in defiance of her circumstances — of her father's failing health.

Darcy wished he had offered to ride to Meryton before Bingley. He had come to Hertfordshire seeking help for his Little Anne, and now Darcy found himself wishing to help Miss Elizabeth.

The thought struck him with a force that stole his breath. He could help her.

Would she accept his assistance if he offered it? He enjoyed her conversation. Her character was strong. She knew when to speak her mind, but Darcy had also witnessed her discretion. She liked children and clearly took the care of her own father seriously.

As quickly as the idea had occurred to him,

Darcy dismissed it. Miss Elizabeth wanted love, not convenience. And Darcy could not deny a good lady her heart's desire.

With a trembling hand, Mr. Bennet reached up to caress his daughter's face.

She closed her eyes, her dark lashes splaying over her cheek. They were as thick as Georgiana's had been, but darker. Almost black. Miss Elizabeth cradled her father's hand between her cheek and shoulder. For a moment, neither of them spoke.

Darcy looked away, allowing them privacy.

How many times he had sat beside Georgiana during her bouts of illness in the mornings, his mere presence the only comfort he could offer her as he held her hair away from her mouth and dabbed her damp forehead with a clean cloth until the nausea subsided. Never had he felt so helpless.

Darcy sat back, the memories aching in his bones.

With a quivering chin and a raspy voice, Miss Elizabeth said, "I wish you had told me you were running out of medicine, Papa. Why did you not tell me?"

"Remember your promise, Lizzy," Mr. Bennet whispered.

A promise.

Darcy looked between the father and his

daughter.

Miss Elizabeth blinked ferociously, but not one tear spilled down her cheeks. Darcy's mind cleared while his vision clouded. They were the same. Darcy did not need to know Miss Elizabeth's promise to be certain she would keep it. At all cost. Just like him. This changed everything. This was his chance.

Stronger, Mr. Bennet said, "Your mother. Your sisters. You must take care of them. You must."

Her voice shook, but her words were clear. "I will not go back on my word, Papa. I will take care of them."

Darcy knew what he must do. It was now or never. "Excuse me for my interference, but if you will allow it, I believe I am in a good position to help."

He felt Miss Elizabeth's glare on him, warming his skin. Her adherence to her own values raised her in his estimation. She would do what was right. She was trustworthy. She was perfect. And she needed him as much as he needed her.

"I wish to sit up," Mr. Bennet said, raising his hand.

Settling in his chair and taking a couple of shaky breaths, Mr. Bennet first appealed to his daughter. "What can it hurt to listen to what Mr. Darcy has to say when he has witnessed our predicament?"

Miss Elizabeth's eyebrows pressed together; her lips flattened into a thin line. She did not argue, but she made her displeasure known, nonetheless. She filled her father's teacup, setting it down with a decided clatter on the tray at his elbow.

Darcy did not blame her. He was not pleased with the circumstances which had brought him to the drawing room at Longbourn either. If there was another way.... But there was not, and wishing things were different would not help Little Anne or Miss Elizabeth. In time, she would see the benefits of his solution.

"More tea, Mr. Darcy?" she asked.

He refused, suspecting she would sooner toss the steaming contents at his face than pour them into his empty teacup. If she already chose to take offense at his offer of help, Darcy held little hope she would take more kindly to his offer of marriage. Not a promising beginning ... but Darcy had begun what he had set out to do, and he would not stop until he was done. He must marry for Anne, and Miss Elizabeth was his choice. There would be plenty of time — a lifetime — for her to change her opinion later.

Mr. Bennet took a sip. Addressing Darcy, he said, "Forgive me for speaking of vulgar topics, but I fear my time is too short for politeness. I must be plain. My estate is entailed, and the gentleman who will inherit Longbourn is eager to take possession of my family's house. I have no reason to believe he will allow my wife and unmarried daughters to continue here when he will soon have a child of his own … and more to come, no doubt. The amount of money I will leave behind is not enough to set my girls up respectably."

Darcy chanced a glance at Miss Elizabeth. Her cheeks were a brilliant red. Her shoulders were hunched up like a cat ready to pounce.

"Some weeks past," Mr. Bennet continued, "I caught a chill which has since turned into this dreadful cough. Not thinking much of it, for nobody dies of a simple cold, I did not seek Mr. Jones' assistance until my cough had become much worse and my throat burned, so that it is painful to swallow. There are times I lose my voice completely. It is a fortnight now that I have been coughing blood." He looked down at the cravat clutched in his hand.

Darcy saw the bright red stain. "Consumption?" he asked. Of all the illnesses….

Mr. Bennet nodded. "I fear my family will be left destitute without me to provide for their needs. My greatest concern is to see my daughters properly settled and cared for."

And so, Mr. Bennet charged the daughter he clearly loved the most with the care of her mother and sisters? Darcy did not know what to think of this frail man. What he demanded was impossible in a society that mocked ladies forced to earn their living. And yet, what other options did Mr. Bennet have at this point? It was too late.

Leveling his eyes at Mr. Bennet, commanding the gentleman's full attention, Darcy said, "I am prepared to make such an offer as to allay your fears, Mr. Bennet. I find myself in need of a wife, and you require a husband to provide for Miss Elizabeth."

Darcy heard Miss Elizabeth gasp, but he did not look away from Mr. Bennet. Once she came to her senses, she would see the advantages of their union. In time, they might even be happy.

Mr. Bennet rubbed his chin. "I know you can provide for her physical needs, Mr. Darcy. You are reported to be quite wealthy."

"You cannot be serious, Papa," Miss Elizabeth cried.

Darcy did not break eye contact with Mr. Bennet. He nodded his head. The reports Mr. Bennet had heard were true.

Neither did the father look away from him. "By your own admission, you do not allow for emotion. Will you be good to her? Will you treat her kindly? Love her as she deserves to be loved?" he asked.

"Papa!" Miss Elizabeth exclaimed. "Do not even

consider this! I will work as a governess. I can ask Uncle Gardiner to allow me to help in his trade. I can keep accounts. Did you not say Aunt Gardiner has relatives who might help? My needs are not grand. I will save all of my earnings to share with Mother and my sisters, only do not do this, I beg you!"

Shaking his head, Mr. Bennet said, "It is only romantic for a gentleman's daughter to earn her living in novels, my dear girl. You do not realize what you would lose."

"And my freedom? What of that? You would allow me to marry a man we do not know? A man who could control me completely and turn back on his promise the moment we are out of your sight? A man who would not value me..." her words cut short.

Darcy's hackles rose, but the tear running down her cheek stole his bravado. Miss Elizabeth was wise to be cautious when she knew so little about him. Composure, not sarcasm, would restore her reason. If she knew how generous he could be with her family, her objections would subside.

Addressing Mr. Bennet, Darcy said, "I will sign a contract promising to provide a residence and a reasonable allowance for your immediate family until they marry. If you require references as to my character, I can provide you with several." Calm enough to face Miss Elizabeth, Darcy turned to her. "As for the authority I exercise over my household, I assure you that I will treat you fairly and kindly, as I do everyone else."

"Everyone else? Do you mean your servants? I should think a wife ought to be treated with a different sort of love and respect to the housekeeper," she snapped.

Mr. Bennet interrupted. "That is enough. You do not agree now, Lizzy, but in time you will see how this is for the best."

"But—"

Her father silenced her. "That is enough. Wishing things were different will not change anything, and if you want your mother and sisters to have any chance of happiness, then sacrifices must be made. I am sorry, but Mr. Darcy is a good man, and he has made an offer we cannot refuse. *I* cannot in good conscience refuse him, and if you have half the sense I know you to possess, you will not either."

Miss Elizabeth stared open-mouthed at her father. Not even when the sound of carriage wheels crunching over the gravel drive drew nearer did she look away.

Her upset was temporary. Tomorrow, she would be grateful.

CHAPTER 9

*E*lizabeth searched her father's face for any sign of remorse. He could not mean it. Surely, he could not.

Heat stung her eyes. Why did he not look at her?

"Sacrifices must be made." He had said that.

"Papa," she muttered.

He did not meet her eyes. Would not.

Did she mean so little to him that he was willing to send her away at the first offer? Elizabeth's eyes flooded with tears she was too angry to allow to fall. How dare he cast her off! What did they know of Mr. Darcy? He could be a monster.

Working herself into a righteous rage, Elizabeth narrowed her eyes at Mr. Darcy. If he had flaws — anything she could use against him to convince her father not to hand her over to the gentleman without pause or consideration — she would find them. Her vision cleared as she inspected Mr. Darcy from the top of his dark, curly hair down his firm jaw; from his perfectly tied cravat and polished boots, then back to his eyes. Were they green or gold?

Mr. Darcy was handsome. Dangerously handsome. Roguishly handsome? No. Elizabeth would never accuse Mr. Darcy of flirting. She could not have foreseen his offer of marriage had her life depended on it.

Her flaw-seeking inspection was not entirely without results. She could not explain why a well-formed, wealthy man like Mr. Darcy was in such a hurry to marry. Neither had he stated his reason clearly. The man had secrets.

Why on earth had he chosen *her*? Not that Elizabeth felt anything was wrong with her, mind you, but she was not so fanciful as to believe that the gentleman before her was her own Sir Knightly, heroically coming to her rescue. It made her wonder what was wrong with *him*. Whatever his great flaw was, it was not visible.

The front door creaked, interrupting her thoughts and breaking her eye contact with Mr. Darcy. Drat it all, how long had she been staring at him?

Mortified, Elizabeth glanced through the window behind her to see Mr. Collins' carriage sitting in the middle of the path to the house. Hill carried in a large trunk. *Good heavens, how long did Mr. Collins plan to stay?*

It was too much.

Elizabeth's ire returned and, with it, a hefty sum of interest for Mr. Darcy's ability to make her forget herself momentarily. She would not allow it to happen again, nor could she stand the sight of her father's envious cousin. If Father so easily threw her future into Mr. Darcy's hands, then he could endure the company of Mr. Collins without her help.

Before an unwelcome foot crossed the threshold, Elizabeth bolted from the room.

Good manners required her to return to the drawing room from whence she had fled, but Elizabeth did not feel at all mannerly. If it were not for Mr. Collins' eager anticipation of Father's death, she would not have to worry about being kicked out of Longbourn. If it were not for her father's untimely illness, he would not be in danger of granting his cousin's wish sooner rather than later. If it were not for Mr. Darcy....

If only she had more time! If only Father had used the time he had better. Then he would not hand her future to Mr. Darcy on a silver platter. Oh, why had he made an offer right when her father was most tempted to accept it? The nerve of him!

It appeased Elizabeth's heart to cast the blame on Mr. Darcy's broad, elegantly dressed shoulders, but she must attempt to be rational. She needed her wits about her if she had any hope of escaping unattached to a man she had only just met.

There were worse fates, she supposed. He was handsome … wealthy … and had offered for her just when such an offer would tempt most ladies.

Once again, suspicion curbed her optimism. Why? Why now? Why her? What was wrong with him?

He would just have to find another wife. She was of age. She was the master of her own destiny. There had to be another way.

She would convince her father to change his mind. He had imbibed three bottles of medicine, meant to last several weeks, in mere days. He was not thinking rationally under the influence of the draught. That was it! Father was drunk. He would have full possession of his senses on the morrow. She would approach him then. And she would have a plan ready when she did.

Pacing the length of her bedchamber floor, Elizabeth considered her options. She could find respectable work as a governess. She loved children, and her uncle Gardiner had many connections with good families through his trade. That was her best prospect.

A tendril of unruly hair fell over her shoulder. Running her fingers down the satin lock, she considered the price her thick waves would fetch. She dropped her hair, letting it fall down the length of her back to her hips. It would grow back. She would not miss it for long.

What price could be put on freedom? On love? Happiness?

Elizabeth wound her hair into a bun, shoving pins into it and begrudging the bleak future contrived upon her by the man who was supposed to protect her interests. Be he intoxicated or not, it still stung.

She would find another way. She had promised to see to the needs of her mother and sisters, and she would honor her word. But she would do it her way. Without Mr. Darcy.

Dropping to her bed, Elizabeth fell back against the covers and smacked her fist against the mattress.

Mr. Darcy was handsome and wealthy, but she did not love him. He did not love her. Without love, what was the point of marriage? Why attach yourself permanently to another unless you craved their company day in and day out? She did not even know if she *liked* Mr. Darcy.

And what of affection? Elizabeth shivered. She refused to believe her first kiss would be a forced one. What else would Mr. Darcy force her to do? She was not a missish maiden. She knew what a husband expected of his wife — an heir and a spare.

She would not give in. She would fight for herself when her own father would not.

"Lizzy?" Jane's sweet voice startled Elizabeth.

Sitting up and smoothing her hair, Elizabeth noticed how the shadows had shifted across the walls. How long had she been in her room?

Jane sat beside her, concern etched across her lovely features. "Are you well? You were pummeling the mattress."

"Fighting against fate," mumbled Elizabeth.

"Since when do you believe in fate?" Jane asked, wrapping her arm around Elizabeth. "Even when things do not go as you wish, you always make the best of it."

She was right, drat it all. Elizabeth believed she was the master of her own happiness. When life gave her sour grapes, she made wine.

Elizabeth tried to rejoice in her sister's joy as Jane described how they had chanced upon Mr. Bingley in Meryton. It was difficult when her own prospects were so easily cast aside. Nor did Elizabeth offer an explanation when Jane mentioned how the gentleman had been in an incredible hurry. Their father's secret was not hers to reveal yet, and Jane's happiness was too lovely to ruin. Mr. Bingley had spared her a smile and a promise to call the following day.

But Jane's reminder gave Elizabeth courage. She would turn her dire situation around. She welcomed the challenge.

Father's illness was nothing more than a challenge. And she would conquer it.

She would speak with him in the morning.

It turned out that fighting an illness was as effective as throwing blows at the air ... or pummeling one's mattress. Father's consumption attacked with full force that night, so that nobody in the household could remain ignorant of its presence.

Mother's nerves confined her to the fainting couch where Kitty attended to her, nearly sending their poor mother into a frenzy every time Kitty coughed.

Mary, not knowing how to comfort anyone, took to her book of sermons when she was not praying.

Jane soothed and placated. Her attentions were required by everyone, and she saw to them without complaint as only Jane could. It pained Elizabeth to see her beautiful sister appear haggard by the following morning.

Mr. Collins practically rubbed his hands together, and Elizabeth hated him more than she mourned her circumstances.

Elizabeth had slept little. Wrestling with her conscience had taken up a good part of the night. She refused to feel selfish for believing her own happiness important, but she possessed more altruism than she had believed herself to have, and it tormented her.

Perhaps her lack of rest was to blame for her impulsiveness. Or, perhaps, it was Elizabeth's resentment toward her father's vulturous cousin. Perhaps it was her own denial of the reality of her new circumstances. Father had not been inebriated when he had accepted Mr. Darcy's offer, nor had he shown any inclination of allowing her to provide for her family's needs in her own way.

Driven by rebellion, justified rage, a need for redemption — there were too many unsavory traits from which to pick — Elizabeth had snapped in the drawing room where her family had gathered with Mr. Collins.

"There is an appalling lack of shelves at Long-bourn, but I am certain my esteemed patroness Lady Catherine de Burgh will generously bestow her opinion on how best to alter the closets. Her lady-ship condescends often to share her views with Charlotte and myself, and I daresay she would not hold back from showing her kindness to you when she learns my poor cousin is on his deathbed."

Is it any wonder Elizabeth's blood boiled at his insensitive greed? She spoke without thought. "If you are so eager to take possession of Longbourn, why do you not spare yourself the trouble of the wait and move in immediately? I daresay Mr. Darcy's estate is large enough to house all of us, so we need not be an inconvenience to you."

She realized her mistake as soon as her mother's eyes lit up like fireworks. "You are engaged? And to Mr. Darcy, no less? Oh, you dear, dear child! We are saved! You knew about this, Mr. Bennet? Why did you not tell me before? Here I have been overcome by nerves when I did not need to worry at all! Is it not the best news?"

Father had not corrected her. His chuckle made Elizabeth go numb.

Finally, he met her gaze directly. His eyes brimmed with gratitude. "Our Lizzy has come to the rescue, and I am thankful to possess such a sensible daughter who is always true to her word. Mr. Darcy offered for her, and he has graciously (and if I might add, quite generously) included the rest of you in his provisions."

There was a collective sigh of relief, and a mind-numbing, flattering speech delivered by Mr. Collins about Mr. Darcy's connection to his imperious patroness.

Elizabeth cursed her spite while she endured the endless praise and compliments of her mother, who proclaimed herself the happiest woman in the kingdom to have such a dutiful, clever daughter.

It was enough to make Elizabeth want to scream. More than once, she cursed her temper. She wished she was the sort of person who could go back on her word. Others did it easily enough. Why could she not? Father praised her for it, but his every compliment stabbed at Elizabeth's back. His betrayal could not have been more complete.

News of her father's consumption spread as quickly as news of Elizabeth's engagement to Mr. Darcy, and the kitchen filled with remedies and concoctions well-meaning neighbors, old friends, and sympathetic tenants left for him. Nobody offered anything to ease the weight in Elizabeth's heart nor the hazy mist fogging her mind. They assumed she must be delighted with her good fortune.

Days passed in a bitter blur, replete with quashing commendation and the burden of her family's expectations. Before Elizabeth could be courted properly, she stood beside the groom to sign her name beside his in the marriage register. For the last time, she signed: Elizabeth Bennet.

She was Mrs. Fitzwilliam Darcy now.

CHAPTER 10

*T*he vows echoed in Darcy's mind. *Wilt thou have this woman to thy wedded wife, to live together after God's ordinance in the holy estate of Matrimony? Wilt thou love her, comfort her, honor and keep her in sickness and in health; and, forsaking all other, keep thee only unto her, so long as ye both shall live?*

He had said, "I do."

When the minister recited the wedding vows, Darcy repeated them.

I, Fitzwilliam Darcy, take thee, Elizabeth Bennet, to my wedded wife, to have and to hold from this day forward, for better, for worse; for richer, for poorer; in sickness and in health, to love and to cherish, till death us do part, according to God's holy ordinance; and thereto I plight thee my troth.

He had a wife.

Darcy looked across the carriage at her. The ring his mother had worn with great pride graced Elizabeth's finger now. The clear blue of the aquamarine stone had been his mother's favorite color. He could not see it with Elizabeth's fist clenched on her lap, but he remembered how easily the ring had slid down her finger.

He had not seen much of her over the past week. It had taken all of his time to acquire the proper license and draw up the contracts to Mr. Bennet's satisfaction. Elizabeth had been more subdued than Darcy had supposed she would be. She had not yet thanked him for coming to her aid, but Darcy was not so necessitous as to require her to. He understood her silence to be a sign of her gratitude.

She stared through the rain-fogged glass, her cheeks in high color. She really was very pleasant to contemplate. Her lips were as plump and red as ripe strawberries. He looked forward to her conversation now that they were alone.

Pulling his handkerchief out of his pocket, Darcy cleared the glass for her.

Turning away from the view, Elizabeth looked instead at him with the same scrutiny with which she had appraised him in Longbourn's drawing room the day he had offered marriage. It was not the appreciative look he had expected.

"We are married now," she said, her eyes lingering on the black opal in his cravat before traveling up to meet his with a resolute glare.

Her look pierced him with displeasure. The curvy lips he had appreciated a moment ago pressed together so firmly, they turned white. Her nostrils flared. She was angry.

"Yes," Darcy said tentatively, covering the opal with his hand. Somber colors were frowned upon at wedding ceremonies, but he needed the reminder it gave him. He wished Georgie could have been there. She would have offered him some insight. She might have explained why his wife seethed with indignation.

What did Elizabeth have to be angry about? He had swept her out of a hopeless plight. She had fulfilled her promise to her father and had nothing more over which to worry. While Darcy did not expect her to be overjoyed, he thought she ought to at least be relieved.

When, after several minutes, Elizabeth showed no signs of casting her ire aside, Darcy took a deep breath and asked, "Is something troubling you?"

"We are married."

He had thought that quite obvious. "Yes."

"I did not want to marry without love."

Frustration fluttered within Darcy. If she did not want to marry, then why had she gone through with it? Why complain now that the deed was done? "And yet you married me. You repeated the vows just as I did."

She scrunched her face and huffed, "Yes, I did," with so much scorn, Darcy became quite offended.

"Why did you go through with it, then?" he asked.

She blinked, sighing deeply. "I said I would do it, and I will not go back on my word. I would have disappointed myself and my sisters ... and I could not have lived with the guilt." Under her breath, she added, "Blast my quick temper and infernal tongue."

Darcy knew better than to smile, but her spicy wording and the reassurance that his choice had indeed been a wise one offered too great a relief to go completely unappreciated. Elizabeth was a lady of her word. Of course, he had known as much. Had he not witnessed her dealings with her selfish father?

He felt her eyes on him, putting an end to his musings.

"I do not even know what to call you. Mr. Darcy?" She shook her head. "No, that is too formal. Husband?" She wrinkled her nose, mumbling, "No, that is too obvious." She narrowed her eyes at him. "Fitzwilliam," she said slowly, nodding as her eyebrow arched and her lips curled sardonically. "Yes, 'Fitzwilliam' will do perfectly when we quarrel. I rather fancy the name right now."

Her humorous remark contrasted so boldly with the tension in the carriage, Darcy guffawed. "My mother used to call me Fitzwilliam when she was cross with me. It did not happen often." He trusted it would not happen often in his marriage either.

Elizabeth folded her arms. "I am not your mother."

Darcy's grin faded. "No, you are not," he mumbled, struck by how distinct the two women were and wishing his mother were still alive. He had not been alone with his wife for a quarter of an hour and, already, he needed the guidance of his matron. He could not be certain, but he began to sense that Elizabeth's anger was somehow directed at him. He could not fathom why.

"It hardly bodes well for us to quarrel on our wedding day. What shall I call you then?" Elizabeth asked.

Finally, she spoke sense. He answered, "Pray call me William."

It occurred to Darcy that he ought to ask how she preferred for him to address her, but she did not give him the opportunity.

"Very well, then, William. Are you a man of your

word? Will you love me or is ours to be a cold, disinterested union?" Elizabeth uncrossed her arms, leaning forward and bracing herself with her hands against the edge of the cushion. She looked as if she would pounce on him if he replied unsatisfactorily.

Her anticipation increased his anxiety while her doubt, once again, injured his pride.

"I always honor my word," he said.

"Forgive me for expressing disbelief, but how can you be so certain? Is it not better to fall in love *before* committing to a permanent union?"

"There was no time. I required a wife, and you required a provider."

"Why did you marry?" she asked.

"I had to."

"Without love?"

Darcy rubbed his hand over his face. "I will provide everything you need."

"Then, it is settled, for I need nothing more than to be cherished, to be of account in an equal union. Now that we are forevermore attached, I should think it is quite obvious that I will look to *you* to satisfy my needs … as you call them."

Where had all the air gone? Darcy pulled at his cravat, but relief was not his to find.

Why could she not ask for gowns and jewels as most ladies would?

He knew the answer as soon as the question crossed his mind. Elizabeth was not like most ladies. He would not have chosen her otherwise.

She bunched her eyebrows together. "Why would you deny yourself love?"

He patted the creases of his cravat until he found the opal. He could not tell her the whole truth yet. How he had been so preoccupied caring for his sister, he had not had time. How he feared he would never be as happy as his parents had once been. How he had failed so badly to keep his family together, all he had now was Anne, and he would die before he lost her too. How he longed to return to how things were when he had a family.

It was too much. It was too soon.

Spinning the opal between his fingers, Darcy weighed his words cautiously. "It is not that I deny myself, but that I do not wish to love again so soon after losing someone very dear to me."

Her eyes searched him, but he had said enough.

After enough time had passed for Darcy to begin to hope Elizabeth's questions had come to an end, she asked, "Why have you not married before now?"

"I have not had time," he repeated.

"Lack of time was not a concern to you when you made an offer for me to my father." Her words dripped with sarcasm.

There being no question, and Darcy not much liking her trail of thought, he did not reply.

But Elizabeth was not content with his silence. More directly, she asked, "Why marry now?"

It was definitely not the time to mention an heir, nor could Darcy speak of Little Anne with so much vitriol in the carriage.

"As I told you, I was in want of a wife."

She scoffed. "If you cannot conjure a better reply than that, then perhaps you can satisfy my curiosity on another point."

Darcy clenched his jaw and peered out of the window. Why were they not yet in London?

"Why me?" she asked.

He locked eyes with her. "Almost from the moment we met, I was impressed with the strength of your character. Even under adversity, you proved yourself loyal and trustworthy ... an estimation I am now beginning to doubt."

Darcy waited for her snappy wit to counter with some comment about how he would not have mistaken her character had he taken the time to court her properly.

He was not prepared to watch Elizabeth's bravado deflate.

Softly, she said, "You are a much more accomplished judge of character than I am. We have been acquainted for the same amount of time, and I know nothing about you."

She looked so fragile against the thick squabs, Darcy regretted his retort.

"Do not underestimate your understanding. Bingley thought your assessment of me rather accurate." When she did not look appeased, Darcy added, "A person whose opinion I trust implicitly spoke favorably of you. It is easier to see proof of the qualities one knows to look for than to discover them without a map."

"I am at an unfair disadvantage then, for there was no one of whom I could inquire about your character other than Mr. Bingley ... and I am of the opinion he speaks kindly of everybody."

She understood Bingley perfectly. However, distrust wrinkled her brow, and Darcy wished to placate her. He wanted to earn her trust. He had to for Anne's sake.

Leaning forward until he had Elizabeth's full attention, he said, "I will always be honest with you. It is true I do not know how I am to be the husband you deserve. I do not know how I can offer you the love you desire when, in my experience, love only leads to a pain so deep one wishes he could stop his heart from beating to keep the ache from consuming him." His throat tightened, so he whispered his assurance. "But I will do my best."

She leaned back against the squabs, her eyes never wavering from his. "I am inclined to believe you, but time will tell whether you mean what you say. In the meantime, William, I will have you know that it is my determination to instigate a thorough study of your character. I wish to love the man I marry, but I will not give my heart away indiscriminately. Not even to you."

He nodded. He expected no less from her. "A fair beginning in our marriage of convenience."

Elizabeth shook her head vehemently. "Forced. Our marriage is not convenient to me at all, and until you convince me it is anything other than a forced marriage, that is how I will continue to think of our union." She laughed bitterly. "I had dreamed of making a love match only to have my dream blown away with one hearty cough. I find myself permanently attached to a stranger. Do not be troubled, William. I have not gone mad. But I will appreciate the ridiculous irony in our situation until I am able to find enough to be happy about, enough hope on which to build a new dream I pray will include you."

Her tenacious search for a silver lining aroused Darcy's sympathy, along with another troubling sensation he did not recognize. Far from being grateful, she was grieving ... because of him.

"I am sorry," he said.

"You do not strike me as a gentleman for whom apologies come easily, and so I will acknowledge the difficulty you have overcome in making one and accept it. It is a point in your favor." She smiled weakly, her forced cheer punching Darcy in the gut and leaving him with the feeling that he had overlooked something important. But what? He had done everything he had said he would do, and more.

His devotion to Anne's protection had narrowed his vision so much, he had failed to consider the complications a wife would add to his already unstable life.

He was a husband now. And he had two females who demanded his attention.

Good God, what had he got himself into?

CHAPTER 11

The expression on William's face should have been enough to make Elizabeth laugh. She dearly loved to laugh, and lately, she had not done much of it. Nor would her streak of laughless days end then. She was too affected, but her fiery courage would rise again. There was too much about William she had yet to learn, and her curiosity would be satisfied.

Elizabeth had to own — if she set aside her own inclination to dislike any man who would marry for anything other than the deepest love — that her husband appeared to be an honorable gentleman. Not Sir Knightly honorable … but few men were. "I do not wish to love again after losing someone very dear to me," he had said.

"Love again." What had he meant by that? Most

society men kept mistresses, and she must admit to the likelihood that William was no different.

As easily as Elizabeth could give in to despair, her optimism insisted he must have a reasonable explanation. She hoped. Something about William moved her sympathy, and Elizabeth realized she stood to lose very little she had not already lost if she indulged it. She may even gain a measure of happiness.

If only he would talk to her.

Why had he needed to marry *now?* He could have had his choice in brides. He could have married a lady of fortune in the first circles of society, but he had chosen her — a country maiden with few aspirations and fewer prospects.

Who had recommended her to him?

Whom had he loved?

Elizabeth brimmed with an endless stream of questions, but she was sufficiently discerning to know when enough was enough. And, right now, William had had enough. *Poor man*, she thought sarcastically. For a gentleman who claimed not to be influenced by emotion, she felt the weight of them in that carriage.

He had said love was painful, that he had wanted to rip his heart from his chest to spare himself the ache.

Was he the sort of gentleman to have a mistress? Elizabeth did not want to believe it. The day was full enough of disappointments to suffer such a soul-crushing revelation so early in the morning.

Please, let it not be another woman. She could turn a blind eye to many things, but not that. Not to betrayal.

She would wait until dinner. Then, she would renew her attempt to learn more about the man she would stick to or be stuck with.

Darcy kept himself occupied until dinner. There were letters to write, invitations to decline, a wife he did not know how to behave around, and observant servants who would carry little bits of gossip past the walls of Darcy House if they suspected anything out of sorts. He was a fair master, but loyalties were often forgotten when a juicy piece of news presented itself. Never forgetting that human weakness had helped him keep Anne secret as long as he had.

Mrs. Fischer, Mrs. Reynolds' sister and the housekeeper at Darcy House, waited for him outside the dining room.

"If I might have a word, please, Mr. Darcy?" she asked.

If she had another task for him to see to, Darcy would be grateful for it. "Anything, Mrs. Fischer," he said.

Her rosy cheeks bunched up. She was plump where Mrs. Reynolds was angular. She was also more outspoken where her sister was tactful.

She said, "That is a promising start and makes my difficulty much easier to utter. I asked one of the maids to assist Mrs. Darcy until she finds someone more suitable."

Elizabeth's lack of a maid had been an unwelcome inconvenience. Mrs. Bennet had insisted that the maid remain at Longbourn, so that her newly wedded daughter could acquire a more fashionable French maid in London. Darcy had sent word as quickly as he could to Mrs. Fischer. Any maid would do until they got to Pemberley.

"Very good, Mrs. Fischer," he said.

Mrs. Fischer frowned, wringing her hands. "With such late notice of Mrs. Darcy's need, I fear it will take several days to find an adequate lady's maid."

"Several days?" Drat! More delay. Darcy held his breath, trying to calm his disappointment. He would not punish Mrs. Fischer when she was only the messenger.

Exhaling slowly, Darcy said, "I can hardly find you at fault when you did not receive the news until yesterday. I thank you for seeing to the comfort of … my wife." His troublesome wife who asked too many questions and delayed his return to Anne. She had almost had him fooled in the carriage. She had inspired his sympathy so greatly, he had apologized. And how did she thank him? By declaring her intention to investigate his character as if he were nothing more than a common criminal out to ruin her happiness. As if she stood a chance of finding happiness at all with such a negligent father, overbearing mother, and complete lack of connections.

Mrs. Fischer beamed. "I aim to have half a dozen lady's maids lined up for Mrs. Darcy to interview by tomorrow — nothing by most ladies' standards, but I am content you are pleased."

Darcy was pleased. They would only lose one day. Elizabeth would simply have to find someone suitable on the morrow. He just had to get to Anne. He had to.

Clasping her hands together, Mrs. Fischer said in a lower voice, "My sister will not agree, but I am overjoyed you chose the second Bennet daughter. She wrote how Mrs. Bamber said that while Mrs. Gardiner adores both of her eldest nieces, the second one seems to be her and her husband's personal favorite. Is Mrs. Darcy as witty as she is said to be?"

At least someone was pleased with his choice. "I do not know the extent of what you have heard, but I am prone to think the reports pale in comparison to the reality."

Patting his hand, Mrs. Fischer bounced on her toes. "I am delighted to hear it! All of us here at Darcy House wish for you to be as happy as your mother and father were."

Doubtful. Darcy guarded his silence, not trusting himself to make an amicable reply.

Before he could continue into the dining room, the source of his affliction appeared at the top of the stairwell. She wore the pale gown with the same green ribbon he had first seen her wear at the Meryton Assembly. Her hair looked as if it would fall out of her pins at the slightest movement — another reminder of her need for a proficient maid. Blast it all.

One day, Darcy reminded himself. Only one extra day in London, then they would hasten away to Anne.

He held out his arm when Elizabeth neared the bottom of the stairs.

She stopped one step from the floor. She did not take his arm but looked at him levelly. "Are you cross, William?" she asked.

Great. Another question.

Heaving a sigh, he said, "No." Now, that was a lie. He had not been married an entire day, and already he was lying to his wife.

She peered at him closely.

Cross or not, he did not wish to begin this way. "I—"

"You are a terrible liar," Elizabeth interrupted. "Your jaw is clenched. I can see the muscles there twitching."

There are few things more irksome than being denied the satisfaction of righting a wrong. Darcy felt his eyelid twitch, annoying him further because he had no doubt that Elizabeth saw it too.

Very well. If she wanted blunt honesty, he would give it to her. "If you must know, I am annoyed about the delay in travel we must suffer due to your lack of a maid."

"So it is my fault, is it? Allow me to soothe over my transgression by suggesting that we leave at first light on the morrow. How could I possibly think we had time to stay in London when we did not even have time to get to know each other in Hertfordshire?"

Darcy did not trust her reasonableness.

Her smile was too sweet. "To be sure, I see no problem in the arrangement ... so long as you are willing to perform the services otherwise seen to by a lady's maid." She reached up to her hair, a tendril falling at the slightest touch. "As you can see, my hair is difficult to manage. Even the most talented maid will be challenged, but I have confidence in your superior abilities."

Darcy knew she was being impertinent, but he was desperate enough to travel on the morrow to consider it. He had seen the groom braid his horses' manes. It could not be that hard.

Elizabeth spun around, her hands fumbling over the buttons at the back of her gown. "Another duty under your charge would be my buttons. I would require your help dressing … and undressing."

Heat crawled up Darcy's neck, flooding his face. This was the woman with whom he was supposed to produce an heir, and right now nothing could provoke him to touch her or her buttons.

She spun back around, facing him. "Are you well, William? You look apoplectic."

He glared at Elizabeth. She had proved her point thoroughly. It was unseemly to rub it in.

Again, Darcy held his arm out for her. His greatest wish was to dine as quickly as decorum allowed and retreat to his study. Away from his contentious wife.

Again, she ignored his gesture.

"You are not given to drink, are you? Forgive me

for asking, but I do not know you well enough to have discovered your vices…"

He jerked his arm away. This woman was insufferable. "I do *not* have vices." He was a Darcy, for Heaven's sake.

She clasped her hand over her heart, reaching to take the arm he no longer offered. "I am relieved to hear it. Most gentlemen — generally speaking, of course — are given to vices, and I could never love a husband without enough strength of character to temper his consumption of spirits … or loose women."

Loose women? Darcy's jaw dropped. "What kind of a man do you think I am?"

"I do not know at all. That is the problem. But we will soon remedy the situation. I have several questions prepared." Elizabeth stepped down off the bottom stair, still holding her hand out expectantly.

He could have used a drink just then, but he could not imbibe in front of her after that comment. Drink was ruined for him. She had ruined it.

Begrudgingly, Darcy gave her his arm and led her into the dining room, wherein she made true to her threat with a barrage of questions.

This was not a celebratory wedding day dinner. This was an inquisition.

CHAPTER 12

*E*lizabeth turned for the maid, holding up her hair so as not to make the difficult task of unhooking the tiny buttons more arduous.

She had overdone it at dinner. She had only meant to make William understand how she wished to be taken into consideration, how she desired to be treated. Whether it was his inability, unwillingness, or his stubborn refusal to grasp her point, Elizabeth did not know, but it did not excuse her behavior. She had yielded to bitterness. William must think her a contemptuous shrew. She felt like one.

In her own defense, how was she supposed to react when time after time Fitzwilliam made decisions without once consulting her? Did her view hold so little value, he thought it best not even to inquire?

They had not been five minutes at Darcy House when she found out they were to continue traveling the following morning. And she had only overheard that comment when Fitzwilliam gave orders to his valet. The valet knew their plans, but Elizabeth did not.

Thank goodness for Mrs. Fischer. She had provided a maid to help Elizabeth bathe and dress for dinner.

Resentful that she would be denied a maid when her husband employed a valet in whom he entrusted more information than herself, Elizabeth had loosened her hair before descending the stairs to dinner, knowing that the slightest movement would send her locks tumbling down.

It had been a long dinner, wherein Elizabeth's every attempt to punish William for his inconsideration resulted in her own shame.

She refused to carry on in this manner. Not only had she made William miserable, but so was she.

Elizabeth sighed. Her misery would not lighten a jot if she insisted on wallowing in it. She must try to see the good ... starting with the housemaid currently assisting her. Perhaps an easier, smaller beginning would help Elizabeth feel more forgiving toward her husband ... and toward herself.

In truth, the girl had done a much better job of

securing Elizabeth's untamable mane than most were capable of doing.

Evelyn — whose untrained fingers lacked the dexterity required of the task before her — tugged on Elizabeth's bodice. "I am sorry," she repeated.

Unwilling to continue in her sour mood, Elizabeth smiled at the girl. "You are doing better than I could manage, Evelyn. Without your assistance, I would be forced to sleep in my gown."

Evelyn chuckled. "My fingers fumble for fear of snagging the fabric — they are quite rough — but Mr. Darcy has arranged for Mrs. Fischer to see about acquiring a proper lady's maid for you. He will see everything is put right."

"Really?" Elizabeth scoffed, biting her tongue. Letting go of her bitterness would be more difficult than she had thought. She smiled at Evelyn.

"Oh, yes. Mr. Darcy sent word before you got here, and Mrs. Fischer has been making inquiries since."

Elizabeth stiffened. She had assumed he had forgotten. Puzzled, she asked, "If he remembered I needed a maid, then why did he arrange to leave for Pemberley on the morrow?"

Another chuckle. "If you ask me, Mr. Darcy loves Pemberley so much, he is simply impatient to show you his grand estate. Who can blame him for wishing to show his beloved home to his bride?"

Elizabeth had blamed him. She still did. "He knew I needed to interview maids," she said.

Evelyn tsked and tugged. "That is a man for you. Mr. Darcy's valet has been in his employ for so long, he has forgotten how much care a lady must take in selecting a proper lady's maid."

Could it be that simple? Had she misunderstood William's impatience as negligence? Elizabeth's shame multiplied. How could she expect her husband to understand her when she clearly did not understand him at all? How could she demand consideration when she herself failed to display the same quality?

She could do better. She would do better. No more confrontational questionings. Until William spoke for himself, Elizabeth would learn what she could from those who knew him and his habits the best — his servants.

Straightening her shoulders, Elizabeth asked, "How long have you worked for Mr. Darcy?"

"My mother was in service to Mr. Darcy's father before me. It was such a happy house. I would not dream of going anywhere else." Elizabeth heard the admiration in Evelyn's tone.

"They sound like lovely people. I am sad I shall never get to meet them."

"Oh, they were lovely. The loveliest!" Evelyn gushed, rewarding Elizabeth's inquisitiveness when she continued. "I was a child when Lady Anne passed away, but I remember her being the most elegant lady I had ever seen. And so friendly. She was not too proud to talk with common folks. Oh, and her gowns! Her gowns were always the height of fashion. The other ladies copied everything she did. If her neckline was square, they rushed to the modiste to have gowns made with square necklines."

Elizabeth stifled a snort. Nobody would rush to copy *her*. Her nicest gowns had been repurposed from Jane's the year when puffier sleeves were all the rage. Her outdated wardrobe was hardly of any consequence at Longbourn, but Elizabeth was in different company now. High society would not be so considerate as her neighbors had been. They would be quick to point out her flaws. *And how can a lady not wearing the latest fashion possibly possess a worthwhile character?* Elizabeth thought sarcastically.

Still, it begged the questions she had been unable to descry at dinner: Why had William chosen *her*? Why not marry within his own circle? Whose opinion did he admire so much, he would marry on their recommendation? What had they said in her praise? The only person of her acquaintance who had a connection to Pemberley was Aunt Gardiner. But that sort of conversation with an unmarried gentleman would not have been overlooked by a dutiful aunt with single nieces, and since her aunt had said nothing of William in her letters, Elizabeth had to assume he spoke of someone else.

Evelyn continued, "Mr. Darcy's father adored the ground Lady Anne walked on. To see those two together, one would never have guessed they had been married over a decade."

Like Lady Gwendolyn and Sir Knightly, Elizabeth thought longingly.

Fishing for more information, Elizabeth said, "It must have been a wonderful place for Mr. Darcy to be raised. There were more children, were there not?"

With one final tug, Evelyn freed the last button. "Aye, it was. Mr. Darcy grieved Lady Anne's loss until his own death. If you ask me, he died of a broken heart. He would have gone much sooner had it not been for Miss Darcy."

A sister! How delightful! Elizabeth listened intently as Evelyn chattered and helped her out of her layers of clothes.

"Miss Darcy was the spitting image of Lady Anne. And her character! So similar the daughter was to her mother, it like to make Mr. Darcy's heart ache at the sight of her."

Elizabeth smoothed the nightdress over her, abruptly reminded that Evelyn was a maid with much more to do than stay and talk with her when the girl said with a curtsy, "Is there anything else I can help you with, Mrs. Darcy?"

"Thank you, Evelyn. I hope we have more opportunity to converse later." Elizabeth could not in good conscience detain her any longer. She had much to ponder though. William had a sister! Why did he never speak of her? Then again, William hardly spoke at all.

"If I may be so bold, Mrs. Darcy," Evelyn said, bobbing another curtsy. "I wish to tell you how happy all of us are downstairs. We feared Mr. Darcy would never marry. And now, he has you, and I think you are lovely."

She spun around and left the room before Elizabeth could recover from her praise. Evelyn had been so full of commendation for the former Darcys, Elizabeth could not help but wonder if the servants would think as kindly of her as they still did of Lady Anne. She determined they would. Already, she had one supporter.

Would William ever grow to love her as deeply as his father had loved his mother? Elizabeth would like that … if he was worthy of her heart. She had learned nothing of import about William other than the fact that he kept a guarded tongue and an accomplished cook. With the day's travel and her own upset, Elizabeth had only managed a few bites. She regretted that now as her stomach grumbled. She might have to find her way to the kitchen. Maybe the cook would be as helpful as Evelyn had been in revealing more about William's past and character.

Elizabeth took a deep breath, straightening her shoulders and lifting her chin. She would not succumb as her father had done. She would not give in to bitterness and despair while she had a lot of fight in her still. This was only the beginning. She would try again. She would do better on the morrow. Better to try and fail than conform to a lifetime of heart-breaking indifference. She was not made for meek resignation or acrimony. She would fight.

Like a queen surveying her domain, Elizabeth assessed her surroundings. She did not know what she sought until she saw it. Her ten-inch bronze hatpin with the green beads.

Grabbing the hatpin off the dressing table, Elizabeth ran her finger along its length to the sharp tip. Yes, it would work perfectly … should she need it.

While Elizabeth was determined to be kinder to her husband, she would not accept unwanted advances from him. She placed it under her pillow.

If William had amorous intentions, she would soon dispel him of them, for Elizabeth refused to lie with a man she did not love.

CHAPTER 13

*D*arcy rose at the first glimmer of daylight. He had slept little, nor would he be capable of rest until he saw Anne. Until she was safe from Wickham.

One more day in London. That was all. He would simply acquire gowns without buttons for his difficult bride.

Dunking his hands in the washbasin, Darcy scrubbed his face. When that did not cool him, he dunked his face in the cold water, letting the beads of liquid run down his neck when he stood. Elizabeth boiled his blood, but she had been his choice. He would live with the consequences of his decisions. What other option did he have? He must do his duty by Anne, and he would try his best to live up to the vows he had made to Elizabeth.

He had few regrets in his life, and he would not hasten to declare his marriage a failure. Not yet. Not after one day.

Dressing without the aid of his valet (really, it was not so impossible as Elizabeth made it seem), Darcy went downstairs in search of Mrs. Fischer. There was a lot to do in preparation for the morrow.

Mrs. Fischer was discussing the menu with Cook when Darcy stepped into the kitchen.

Cook, her cheeks as red as apples from the exertion of kneading the dough on the table, wiped her dusty hands on her apron. "Master Darcy come to visit me in the kitchen again? Well, this is a treat! Will you have a scone with a spot of preserves?"

Darcy was stunned. "You have extra this early in the morning?"

Cook beamed. "I always save a few when the master is in the house, knowing your weakness for sweet things," she said, hobbling over to the pantry and returning with a scone and a jar of red berry preserves.

In a blink, Darcy was twelve years younger. He and Georgiana had crept downstairs to invade the pantry where Cook always saved treats for them. Strawberry tarts had been Georgiana's favorite. They would whisper and shush each other, huddling around a candle, and Darcy would help Georgiana wipe the evidence of their activities from her sticky face and fingers until she was old enough to perform the service herself. The memory was so real, and it gripped Darcy so hard, he struggled to swallow his bite.

Fortunately, Cook twirled away from him, mumbling something about chocolate.

Sitting opposite Mrs. Fischer at the table, Darcy soon found himself surrounded with more food than he could possibly consume in a week.

Mrs. Fischer leaned forward and whispered. "She will empty the larder unless you start eating. Just yesterday, she declared you far too thin for your strong build."

Cook emerged from the pantry, hefting a ham as large as the soup pot bubbling on the range.

Darcy shoved the scone into his mouth before she produced anything else.

Cook grinned. "Ah, now that is more like it. You will need your strength if you are to fill this house with children."

Darcy choked.

"Martha!" exclaimed Mrs. Fischer.

Pounding his chest and coughing, Darcy took the cup Cook shoved at him. The chocolate scalded his lips and burned a molten path down his throat, making his eyes water.

"What? Any young lady would be blind not to want to receive the attentions of such a fine, good man," Cook continued.

Blurry eyed and gasping for breath, Darcy coughed again. She would be the death of him if the subject was not changed quickly.

"Martha, it is bad enough you insist on calling him Master Darcy when he is no longer a child, but it is hardly appropriate for you to discuss Mr. Darcy's personal affairs," Mrs. Fischer chided.

With a wink that lit Darcy's skin afire, Cook said, "Mrs. Darcy is a handsome lady with a tooth for sweet things, too. I had the pleasure of feeding her last night. She came tip-toeing into the kitchen just like Master Darcy used to do. She is everything charming and lovely."

Not the words Darcy would have used to describe his wife…. Wait … why could Elizabeth be good-natured to the cook and not to him?

Nodding her head, Cook added with another wink, "Mark my words, we will hear a child's laughter at Darcy House within the year!"

Mrs. Fischer rolled her eyes. "Oh, bake your bread and hold your tongue, or have you completely forgotten your place?"

Cook did not seem the least bit worried about

her place, but she returned to the mounds of dough resting on the table.

Darcy took a deep breath, trying to calm his heated complexion and cool his seared tongue.

"You know what would be romantic?" Mrs. Fischer said, resting her chin against her palm and looking at him.

Romance was hardly on Darcy's mind. All he wanted to do was leave for Pemberley. Was that too much to ask?

The meddling housekeeper continued without any encouragement from him.

"You ought to take a tray up to Mrs. Darcy's bedchamber. I do not know a woman alive who does not appreciate her husband bringing her breakfast in bed."

Darcy thought it prudent to avoid his wife's bedchamber.

Ignoring Mrs. Fischer's suggestion, Darcy asked the question for which he had sought her out. "Were you able to arrange several interviews today?"

"Oh, yes. There are a couple of promising applicants, but only Mrs. Darcy will be able to discern who will suit her best. Not just anyone will do as a lady's maid. And as you know, we have other..." Mrs. Fischer dropped her voice to a whisper, "...concerns which require discretion and trustworthiness."

Darcy cradled his hands around his chocolate, but the steaming liquid did not warm them. It would be difficult to keep Anne secret from a lady's maid. They were usually privy to the family's most intimate affairs.

Pulling out a letter from her apron pocket, Mrs. Fischer handed it to Darcy. "This arrived from my sister yesterday. I did not read it until after retiring from my duties or else I would have shown it to you earlier. Open it and read the last page."

Darcy did as she bid, his eyes skimming over Mrs. Reynolds' tidy handwriting until he saw his name.

She wrote: *Pray inform Mr. Darcy that the filly is doing well.*

"Filly" was their code word for Anne. Should their letters be intercepted, nobody would raise more than a curious eyebrow at a foal born so late in the year.

He continued reading.

Like all young things, she is content so long as she has food and company. Mr. Darcy will not take my suggestion, but your tongue is bolder than mine, and so I will leave you to convince him to stay in London for at least a fortnight — a month if you can manage it.

Impossible! Out of the question.

Disgruntled, he read on, determined that whatever arguments Mrs. Reynolds presented, his answer would remain unchanged.

The filly will not notice his absence of a fortnight. You will convince him, I trust. It is not in his nature to use others to his advantage as Mr. Wickham used Miss Darcy, and I cannot allow he will use the young lady he married in such an ill manner either.

That was all there was, but had there been more, Darcy's eyes would not have moved beyond that last paragraph.

Use others to his advantage as Mr. Wickham used Miss Darcy. Darcy's stomach soured in disgust. Mrs. Reynolds compared him to Wickham? To a man so intent on gaining the fortune and position he believed to be his, he had abused Georgiana — neglecting her and exposing her to his self-serving indifference while Darcy watched her heart break?

They were nothing alike! He shoved the letter across the table.

Why should he extend his stay in town? What did town offer that Pemberley could not over-shadow? Surely, Elizabeth would feel more comfort-able in the country than she would in London society.

"Pardon me for interfering," began Mrs. Fischer in a tone which implied no remorse and every incli-nation of continuing whether he wished for her to or not. "But have you discussed the matter with Mrs. Darcy?"

"No." What was there to discuss? Anne needed him more than Elizabeth needed a maid.

Mrs. Fischer continued, "London is an exciting place for a lady accustomed to the quiet of the country. I imagine she would like for you to show her around."

Darcy imagined no such thing.

Mrs. Fischer must have discerned his disagreement, for she changed tactics. "It would be a kindness to your wife to see to her wardrobe during your stay. The families in your circle will not take the news of your matrimony well — especially the ladies who have tried, and failed, to capture your attention over the years. They will use anything they can against Mrs. Darcy."

"Why would she wish to be friends with those malicious females?" Darcy did not waste his time on them, and he could not imagine why Elizabeth would want to either.

Mrs. Fischer sighed. "She will need your help to ease into society. A favorable first impression will serve her well in the years to come."

Darcy frowned at Mrs. Fischer. So much for not interfering in his personal matters.

The housekeeper was not done voicing her opinions yet. She said, "Aside from a new wardrobe, you ought to take her for a drive in Hyde Park. Take her to the theater and out for ices. It is the least you can do for what you expect of her."

Again, Darcy's face burned. He could not deny the truth in Mrs. Fischer's reminder. He needed an heir, and thus far, he had not done a very good job encouraging affection in his wife. If anything, she despised him.

In truth, he despised himself. The longer he waited to confide in her, the harder it would become. And yet, he could not bring himself to tell Elizabeth the entire, awful truth, knowing she wanted more than he was capable of giving. It was difficult to think of love when a defenseless child depended on him at Pemberley. A child he was powerless to keep from Wickham without Elizabeth's help. He needed her. He must not forget it.

Drat. Darcy rubbed his hands over his face, hating how the only solution would keep him from Anne.

"Pack a hamper. I am taking Mrs. Darcy for a drive in the park." He would prove he was nothing like Wickham, or his name was not Fitzwilliam Darcy.

CHAPTER 14

*M*rs. Fischer rose from the table. "I had best see the breakfast parlor is in order. Country folks keep earlier hours, and I suspect Mrs. Darcy will wake soon if she has not already."

Cook bustled about collecting dishes, complaining, "I hope Mrs. Darcy does her plate better justice than you do." Unloading the contents of her arms into the pantry, she crossed them and watched Darcy.

Surely, she did not expect him to eat again after the spread she had just laid out for him. Other than a scone and half a cup of chocolate, he had not consumed much. Certainly not enough to satisfy Cook.

"Well? Does she?" Cook asked.

It took Darcy a moment to catch on, and his relief was only brief when he realized Cook inquired about Elizabeth's appetite and not his lack of one. He had not the faintest notion how to reply. Neither he nor Elizabeth had eaten much the night before. Her slight build suggested that the propensity of her stomach was bound to disappoint Cook.

Grabbing a piece of ham before she put the tray away, Darcy popped it into his mouth both to appease her and to avoid having to give an answer. He knew so little about Elizabeth, and he had not revealed much of himself to her. They were strangers. Married strangers.

Washing down his bite with the rest of his cooled chocolate, Darcy made his way up the hall.

Voices from the direction of the breakfast parlor suggested that Mrs. Fischer had been correct in assuming Elizabeth would arise early. Darcy followed the sound, stopping short when he saw his bride tugging at one end of the velvet drapes at the window.

"Such a lovely view of the garden to cover with thick draperies. Pray help me move the table closer to the window. One must never miss an opportunity to appreciate nature where there is so much less of it to see in town," she said to the maid, biting her bottom lip as she tugged at the fabric and watched with wide eyes as the stiff yellow silk moved across the rod holding it up. Elizabeth looked as charming and vivacious as Darcy remembered her being at the Meryton Assembly. It was a welcome sight.

The maid's eyes widened when she saw him leaning against the door frame. Rushing over to Elizabeth, she took the drapes from her. "Let me help you with those, Mrs. Darcy."

Elizabeth took notice of him, too. Her eyes roved over his face, and she smiled nervously. "What do you think, William?"

He was pleased to be "William" that morning. Last night, he had been "Fitzwilliam."

She stepped toward him. "Shall we look over the garden while we break our fast together?" Clasping her hands, she added, "That is, if you are agreeable to the idea. After last night, I would not blame you if you do not wish it … but, I should very much like to try again."

Remembering her words from the carriage the day before, Darcy said, "I recognize the effort with which you extend a white flag, and I accept it. It is a point in your favor." His lips twitched.

Hers did too. "We are even, then, both in our

merits ... and our demerits. I would much rather focus on your better qualities in the hope you will extend me the same courtesy."

"Naturally," he said with a bow.

Their truce thusly made, Darcy joined her by the window expecting to see an array of spring flowers. All he observed were bare branches and empty flowerbeds.

"There is hardly anything worth seeing," he commented.

Elizabeth touched the glass with her fingertips. "Is not the grass gloriously green? Nobody notices it in the spring when there are so many flowers competing with it for attention. Green is my favorite color."

Standing as she was against the green backdrop reflecting through the windowpane, Darcy appreciated how the color complemented Elizabeth's rich chestnut hair, the pink in her cheeks, and the creamy brown of her eyes. Green suited her. He knew her favorite color — an insignificant detail, one might argue, but at that moment, it felt important to Darcy. It was a beginning.

What would she think of Hyde Park, with the ladies preening and posing in their carriages like hothouse flowers? They cared not for the beauty around them. Their purpose was entirely vain-glorious.

What would Elizabeth think of Pemberley? Would she prefer it, as he did, to town? He hoped so. How he missed his little girl.

A brief parting in the clouds bathed the room in sunlight, and Elizabeth raised her shoulders as she closed her eyes, soaking in the warmth with a sigh. Contentment suited her.

Seeing his wife in the full light of day, Darcy appreciated how the wave of her hair was evident despite the obvious attempts to tame it. Tiny curls, as fine as Anne's baby fine hair, defied the pins and braids around her forehead and at her temples. Light freckles spattered across her cheeks and nose, another proof of her societal rebellion. She smelled of lavender. His favorite.

Would she protect Anne as he did? Would she be a kind mother?

Shadows fell over them, bringing a chill, and Elizabeth opened her eyes before Darcy thought to look away.

"You do not fear the sun's effect on your complexion?" he asked, wishing he could have spouted a cleverer comment rather than a stupid question. Of course she did not fear the sun. Most ladies of his acquaintance, however, did. They hid behind closed curtains inside their houses for fear of marring their porcelain skin. Like bats in their caves.

Her laugh was reply enough, and Darcy was glad for it. The glories of Pemberley lay in its carefully maintained grounds and the wild forests beyond. Impressive as the house was, it simply could not compare to the nature surrounding the structure. Mrs. Bamber was right to regret Anne's inability to see it. She ought to be free to roam over the fields as he and Georgiana had.

"I have only to look out of doors to remember how fortunate I am to live and breathe and move freely," Elizabeth said, her smile fading as their eyes met.

Did she think he would take away her freedom? Granted, she considered their marriage forced, but Darcy did not wish for Elizabeth to think him selfish or cruel. He was *not* Wickham. He would prove it to her.

Remembering Mrs. Reynolds' letter, Darcy said, "It would be my pleasure to take you for a drive in Hyde Park. Then, perhaps, we will stop at the dress-maker to see about a new gown ... if you wish." He wanted to make certain she knew she had a choice.

"I would like that very much," she said through a grin that shone in her eyes. Elizabeth reminded

Darcy of a bottle of champagne — bubbling with energy and sparkle.

He found himself returning her smile, and for the first moment since he had departed from Pemberley, he was not quite in such a hurry to return.

CHAPTER 15

There was a bite to the wind only the most intrepid lovers of the open air braved to endure. Darcy was prepared to cut their drive through the park short before the heated bricks at their feet cooled, but Elizabeth surprised him when she patted the seat beside her and suggested they share their warmth.

At first, Darcy gloried in her pleasantness. She was the woman he had known her to be. His instincts had been correct. He had not chosen foolishly.

However, the more Elizabeth smiled and exerted herself to keep their conversation light, the heavier Darcy's secrets became. Darcy's sense of justice could not allow for Elizabeth's effort to go unrewarded, nor could he ignore his unfairness in holding his silence. But neither would he punish her kindness by revealing the truth. He needed an heir. How cold that sounded! He did not want to keep secrets from her, but how could he tell her without being cruel?

Elizabeth looked up at him and smiled, her pupils dancing and the corners of her eyes crinkling. She looked happy.

It was the first time Darcy had seen her smile since the Meryton Assembly. He could not take the moment away from her.

His mind went blank, unable to settle on a light topic when graver matters loomed between them. *Soon*, Darcy appeased himself. He would tell her soon. Just not today. Not yet.

Darcy looked around, observing the riders in the park more intently.

One could always discern when the fashionable ladies of the *ton* (who preferred the entertainments in town over the quiet of their fathers' and husbands' country estates) had acquired a new gown. They paraded by in droves, immune to the chill, in favor of displaying their new designs for all to admire and envy. They were ridiculous — with towering feathers poking out of hats tilted at impossible angles and held together by Lord-knew-what. Darcy prayed Elizabeth had better taste.

He pointed one such example out to Elizabeth. "What do you think of her bonnet?" he asked.

"She will not be easily lost in a crowd," Elizabeth commented as the lady rode past them with an ostrich feather billowing above her head.

Darcy mumbled, "She might fly away."

Elizabeth chuckled. "The first known ostrich to take flight? No, I would not deny the birds their plumage for my own vanity. My taste is much simpler."

More than a little relieved at her reaction — for many a country maiden had been known to adopt garish fashion to display their newfound wealth — Darcy said, "Grace and elegance are beautification enough."

She wrinkled her nose. "I will not claim to possess either quality, but neither am I blind to my strengths. If you, for example, propose a debate, I will hold my ground against you. Unless, of course, we are in accord. Then, I would have to applaud your reasonableness. Relationships are far more agreeable when all parties are in union, are they not?"

Darcy laughed. "That is one point on which we seem to be in complete agreement, though I would argue on your behalf. I consider your own estimation of your grace and elegance rather stingy," he said, proud that Elizabeth possessed a healthy, humorous wit and nervous to learn her turn of thought. His aunt Lady Catherine de Bourgh was known for her strong opinions, but Darcy never agreed with her.

Elizabeth's eyes sparkled as she laughed. "If I am tempted to address you as 'Fitzwilliam' this fortnight, I shall remember that comment and forget why I was cross."

"Only a fortnight?"

She shrugged. "Flattery does not last beyond a week, but a genuine compliment, so smoothly delivered, deserves twice the duration."

Darcy chuckled. His breath puffed in icy bursts, but he was not cold.

Elizabeth tilted her chin upward, granting Darcy a perfect view of her eyes. "You know my favorite color, but I do not know yours," she said.

"Chocolate," he replied. He had never given the matter much thought before then, but he could say with absolute certainty that he favored the tone.

She raised her eyebrows. "For a pair of boots or breeches, maybe. But for a waistcoat?"

"You do not accept my reply?"

Elizabeth poked his arm. "You forget, sir, that I have an inquisitive mind and, until recently, not enough to stimulate it. My powers of perception are well trained through use. I may not be able to puzzle the complete truth, but I can almost always spot when something is off balance. You replied much too quickly for your answer to be the truth, and so I must suppose that while impulse (or hunger) moved you to respond as you did, chocolate is not your real favorite."

Darcy's stomach felt heavy. Was Elizabeth really so perceptive?

She blinked up at him, waiting for his real reply.

He had always favored blue, it being his mother and sister's favorite color, but the image of Elizabeth standing in front of the windowpane in the parlor that morning was not one he would soon forget. "Blue, although I have developed a deeper appreciation for green of late."

She settled against the cushion, her side pressed against his. "Blue is so calm and serene. Attributes I shall never possess, I fear. I hope you do not expect me to be complacent and peaceful all the time," she teased.

"What if I did?" Darcy teased in turn.

"Then you should prepare yourself for the moment I lay my expectations of *you* bare, for I refuse to carry the burden of our union's happiness alone."

Darcy was uncertain how to reply to her challenge. He, too, wished to be happy. But he dared not hope it was possible. Too much could go wrong — had gone wrong — for him to believe it could happen twice in his lifetime.

Her smile returned. "And that is enough serious talk from me. I am determined to be pleasant, and I will not allow for anything to ruin this glorious day."

An easterly wind whipped around the carriage, piercing through the warmth of the blanket covering their legs.

Darcy looked down the serpentine path, his heart sinking like a stone. He blinked heavily, wishing he would wake from a nightmare rather than face the ruiner of his family's happiness. The man was still there. Darcy's fists clenched and his heartbeat thrummed in his ears. Of all the people they should cross in the park, they had to see *him*.

The blackguard in the carriage opposite was not alone. Rogues seldom were.

He sat next to a woman donning a gray mourning gown cut low enough over her bust to suggest that any sadness she had felt for her loss was long gone. The jewels she draped over her exposed skin, large enough to see even at a distance, professed her status as a wealthy widow. Wickham would not bother for anything less.

He had removed the mourning bands from his hat and coat already ... if he had worn them at all.

Georgiana deserved so much better.

There was no way to avoid passing them, but Darcy's driver was trained well. He raced by them at a cheek-reddening clip without a word from Darcy. Precious few servants in his household knew about Anne, but they all knew his estimation of George Wickham.

They could not stay in Hyde Park. And now that Darcy knew Wickham was in town, they could not stay much longer in London either. Wickham would delight in filling Elizabeth's mind with poison against him, and she was inquisitive enough to listen. Georgiana had. And now, she was gone. And Anne was without a protector at Pemberley.

Tapping against the driver's box, Darcy said, "Carry on, please. To Madame Givenchy at Cavendish Square. Wigmore Street." How badly he had wanted to direct the driver to Pemberley. To his little girl.

One maid and one gown. One week if he paid handsomely. Then, nothing would prevent him from returning to Anne.

CHAPTER 16

*E*lizabeth craned her neck around to catch one final glimpse of the man in the other carriage. Who was he? It was plain he and William had a history. She died to know what it was.

William had not spared a second glance at the saucy widow clinging to the gentleman — to Elizabeth's immense relief. Though he had denied such vices, his earlier comment of not loving again haunted her. Whomever he had previously loved, Elizabeth was certain it was not the widow in the carriage. The lady was a study in contrasts with her gray gown and flashy jewels. If her intent was to call attention to herself, she had succeeded marvelously. Outside the fashion plates Lydia pored over, Elizabeth had never seen such a revealing bodice. The necklace the lady wore provided her only modicum of modesty, and Elizabeth had been hard put not to stare at the unusually cut diamonds — rounded squares shaped like pillows — nestled at the widow's bosom.

William was quiet. Quieter than he had been coming from Longbourn — a feat Elizabeth would not have believed possible from anyone but him.

It was a pity. She had been enjoying his company.

The muscles at his jaw twitched, and his lips pressed together in such a way as to discourage conversation. But Elizabeth was not easily dissuaded … though she would proceed with greater care this time. She had learned from her mistake the night before.

Keeping her tone soft, she asked, "Who was that man?"

"George Wickham."

She waited several minutes, but William said nothing more. George Wickham was an interesting name, but it did not signify anything to her.

"I suppose from your cut that he is not a friend?" she prodded.

William snapped, "He is the worst man I have ever had the displeasure of knowing."

Now, she was more curious than before.

After what felt like an eternity, whereupon William offered no further explanation, Elizabeth said, "You will have to expand on that unless you wish me to believe what my wild imagination can conjure."

Nothing. The muscles in William's jaw flinched, and his firmly set lips might as well have turned to stone for all the answers she would get.

Frustrated that the mere sight of Mr. Wickham had marred their cheerful morning, that her pleasantness had not loosened William's tongue at all, Elizabeth tried to dissipate the murky cloud enveloping her husband in silence before irritation overwhelmed her determination to be agreeable. She was unwilling to repeat her performance of the night before, but neither would she accept more of William's reticence.

Flippantly, she said, "Very well. I will believe him a murderer who selfishly gambles with the hopes of innocent maidens; a villain who leaves a trail of grief wherever he goes."

William's skin paled and he swallowed hard.

Elizabeth's eyes widened. She had been referring to Lady Gwendolyn's evil stepbrother, a melodramatic character of fiction, not anyone real.

"You would not be far from the truth," William said, the color slowly returning to his cheeks.

"Oh." Elizabeth was afraid to say anything more. She supposed such wicked people existed, but she had never crossed paths with one. One thing was certain: The cost of satisfying her curiosity was too great. She would bide her time … and learn what she could from other sources. What would Evelyn have to say about Mr. Wickham?

Finding solace in her plan, Elizabeth said, "I dislike him more than anyone already. If I should cross paths with him again, I, too, shall give him the cut direct."

William's hazel eyes bore into hers; his nostrils flared. "You must not ever speak with him."

Had she not said as much? Was William not listening? Elizabeth's rebellion arose. Did he expect her blind obedience when he gave no reason for her to submit to it?

His stern demeanor did not crack. Turning and leaning closer to her so that he filled her vision, he said in a tone that brooked no argument, "Promise me you will stay away from him."

Elizabeth raised her chin, all the better to return his glare. Was Mr. Wickham the reason William had insisted they leave for Pemberley so soon after their wedding? Had he wished to avoid London for fear of seeing him? What was William hiding from her that Mr. Wickham might expose?

More than ever, Elizabeth wanted to speak with the gentleman, but another chance encounter with him was unlikely. It was much too crowded in town. Drat it all.

Shaking his head and rubbing his hands over his face, William leaned back against the carriage squabs. "I apologize. I cannot make demands when I have given no explanation. I will explain. Only, not now. Please—" his voice cracked, and he went silent.

Elizabeth's defiance melted away, yielding to sympathy.

Worry lined William's face and pinched his features. Would she ever understand him? He claimed not be ruled by emotion, but his reaction to Mr. Wickham had been visceral, moved by deep agitation. Much as his offer of marriage to her had seemed. But she would not describe William as impulsive. How would she describe him?

For every answer Elizabeth sought, a dozen more questions arose.

She had married a walking conundrum.

Elizabeth's pondering soon came to an end when they arrived at a fashionable shop with a large glass window bursting with bright colors and textures begging to be touched.

"Monsieur Darcy!" exclaimed an elegant French-woman with silver hair piled high on her head. Her coiffure might have been from the last century, but the dainty lace overlay she wore over shimmering purple satin was unlike anything Elizabeth had seen before. The Vandyke points on her sleeves were awe-inspiring.

William took the woman's hand, bowing over it while she basked in his attention. He introduced Elizabeth to Madame Givenchy, the proprietress of the establishment.

Elizabeth fell under the kind scrutiny of Madame Givenchy, who circled around her as her smile grew. Finally, when she had come full circle, she clapped her hands. Addressing William, the woman said, "She is a striking contrast to your mother and sister. I shall be able to adorn Mrs. Darcy with all the bold colors with which I dared not dress them. Oh, she is lovely!"

Elizabeth released her breath. She liked this woman.

At the snap of Madame's fingers, a seamstress, who had been studying a drawing at the counter, scurried over to them.

"Do you not think a wide neckline would show Mrs. Darcy's swanlike neck to better advantage? And her sleeves ... she does not need the puff," Madame Givenchy tsked thoughtfully.

Resisting the urge to touch her neck — nobody besides Jane had ever flattered her features before — Elizabeth hung onto Madame's every word.

She, however, needed to make one point clear. "Not too wide … or too low," Elizabeth said, recalling the woman in the park.

Madame smiled. "I reserve the — shall we call them … revealing — designs for the ladies who ask for them. They do not have faces like yours and so must draw attention to their other attributes."

Elizabeth liked Madame Givenchy very much. She liked the pink tinge she saw in William's cheeks every time Madame looked to him for his opinion. Their eyes met several times, and Elizabeth felt her own cheeks blush.

The older woman continued, "One of Mrs. Darcy's gowns must fall like the petals of a tulip…." She spoke under her breath in French while her seamstress counted on her fingers all the details the proprietress expected her to remember.

So enraptured was Elizabeth, William's voice was a jolting intrusion. "We have one obstacle which I pray you will help us surmount, Madame. My confidence would be lost on another, but I know you are capable of great things when you are decided."

"*Oui*, you remember me well. I delighted in dressing your mother, and I will do no less for your wife, Mr. Darcy. What is this obstacle I must help you overcome?"

"We must return to Pemberley in no more than a week."

Elizabeth's eyes snapped to William at the same time Madame Givenchy exclaimed, "*Impossible!* That is not sufficient time for one gown, much less a wardrobe."

"One is sufficient until we are able to return. I must beg your understanding. There is an urgent matter waiting for my attention. Our attention," William corrected himself, his eyes flickering to Elizabeth.

What did he mean by this? She did not know whether to be happy he included her or upset he had changed their plans once again without consulting her.

Madame brushed him off with a wave of her wiry hand.

"Nonsense. If Mrs. Darcy did not have a trousseau made before her wedding day, then she ought to have one now. She is a Darcy. I will make her the most beautiful lady in England, and all the wives will wish they had such attentive husbands as hers."

Elizabeth wished she knew what to make of William's attentions. There were moments he made her madder than she had ever been, and then there were moments like the assembly and that morning when she really felt they had a chance at happiness together. This swaying back and forth was exhausting.

"Let me see you together," Madame Givenchy said, grabbing Elizabeth by the shoulders and moving her with a shocking amount of strength over to stand by William.

Their sleeves brushed, sending tingles running like shivers out to Elizabeth's fingertips and toes.

Stepping back and pinching her chin, Madame frowned. "Closer. There is no need for this distance. You are married, *oui*? Your father, he never lost an opportunity to embrace your mother."

William moved behind Elizabeth. If she tilted her weight back slightly, she'd rest against his chest. The perfect height to hear his heartbeat. That she was tempted to lean back warmed her through.

"*Mon dieu*, she is your wife! Embrace her! I need to see how you fit so that I may create my best design.

William's arm wrapped over Elizabeth's shoulder and around her waist. He was warm and solid, and she fitted perfectly into the crook of his shoulder. Her skin felt every brush of fabric, and she wondered if it were possible to melt when his fingers rested at the top of her hip.

She draped her arm over his as naturally as if

they were lovers and nestled against him until his posture stiffened. William's heart beat as wildly as hers did. Elizabeth could hear it.

Madame walked around them, oblivious to what she had done. "Yes, you are the perfect match. You must have silk gowns in deep purple, robin's egg blue, resplendent green … aside from her riding habits and morning gowns … and perhaps a little something special I can stitch together for the night, *oui*?" she added with a suggestive arch of her brow.

William jumped away, crossing his arms over his chest and leaving Elizabeth perturbed at her own reaction to his nearness.

She wrapped her arms around her torso and thought about the hatpin under her pillow. Even worse than the thought of William coming to her bedchamber that night was the thought that he did not wish to come at all. What hope did she have of understanding him when she did not even understand herself?

Elizabeth shook her head. No, the hatpin would remain until she knew William enough to know herself in love with him. She would be greatly disappointed in him were he to try to induce her to love him before she was ready.

Madame snapped her fingers, and several books appeared on the counter. Elizabeth focused on the dressmaker, thinking that safer than her own thoughts. And she was partly right. Madame flipped through the drawings, commenting briefly on which details she thought would accentuate Elizabeth's features while her seamstress took notes as quickly as she could write.

Elizabeth had never considered herself vain, but through Madame's assessment, she gained a new appreciation for her thick, shiny hair, her slender frame, and her sun-kissed skin. Not one feature was seen in a negative light, but, rather, it was meant to be accentuated. Every comment Madame uttered lifted Elizabeth up in her own estimation until the woman would have had her believe she was a great beauty.

The way William looked at her before acquiescing to some of the elderly woman's demands warmed Elizabeth from the inside out. He was not so indifferent as he had led her to believe, and she basked in the warmth of his regard.

And, so, it was decided. Elizabeth would get a full wardrobe from top to bottom. Madame ensured William knew the best places to complete her ensembles with the proper bonnets, slippers, fripperies, and even jewels to wear with her gowns. Elizabeth tried to pay attention, but it was overwhelming.

When, hours later, Elizabeth departed from the shop, she overheard William's only request. "I give you *carte blanche*, Madame. There is only one favor I will ask. Finish the green within the week."

"I cannot convince you to extend your stay?" Madame asked yet again.

"It is nonnegotiable."

Madame sighed, then purred, "The green is an excellent choice. She will look like a goddess of the forest, a queen of the emeralds."

A part of Elizabeth — the romantic part that dared to hope she was so fortunate as to marry a good man worthy of her heart despite their rough beginning — softened to allow for an improved opinion of her husband. It was easy enough, for she wanted to think well of him. But she knew the danger of the game she played and prayed he would not prove false to her hope. Elizabeth did not know if she could bear another betrayal.

For now, though, for this moment, it was enough. William had remembered her favorite color.

CHAPTER 17

*W*hile Evelyn was a valuable source of information regarding the Darcys, she was remarkably close-lipped when Elizabeth mentioned Mr. Wickham's name.

Looking about and dropping her voice to a whisper, Evelyn had said, "Mr. Wickham is not to be spoken of here. He is a very bad man."

"Do you know him?" Elizabeth had asked.

Evelyn shook her head, her eyes wide. "I do not, nor would I wish to know the man who has caused more suffering to the Darcys than any other."

That was all Elizabeth could get from the girl, nor did she have greater success the following day when she casually mentioned his name in conversation with Mrs. Fischer and Cook. Both of the women had gone silent.

Elizabeth had no other option but to wait impatiently for her husband to tell her why Mr. Wickham's name was treated like a curse at Darcy House. She would not hold her breath.

Two days had passed since their chance meeting at the park, and while William did not inspire her trust (he had too many secrets for that), he did encourage Elizabeth's respect. Not once had he knocked on her bedchamber door. Her hatpin lay untouched under her pillow where it would remain until he deemed her worthy of his confidence.

That morning, she found William sitting in the breakfast parlor. He drank coffee at the table she had pulled closer to the window, a pile of platters worthy of a small regiment lined up on the sideboard. His hair was still damp from the attentions of his valet. Elizabeth liked how the ends of his hair curled over his collar.

She liked, too, how he poured her a cup of coffee and set it at the place to his right as she walked into the room. He even added two scoops of sugar and a dollop of milk. He had been paying attention. That was exactly how she preferred her coffee when sugar was to be had.

Filling her plate, Elizabeth joined him. "Are we expecting company for breakfast or is this Cook's way of telling you to eat more?"

William smiled. "Did you rest well?"

Two days of interviews, fittings, and riding around London in search of bonnets, slippers, and other fripperies had been fun for the first few hours. Not so much the entire following day. Elizabeth was tired of ribbons and lace, and yes, she was even tired of the jewels. She sat beside him, saying, "Well enough. And you?"

He held up his cup, saluting the air with it. "This is my third cup."

William's brow creased as he set down his coffee, staring into the dark, steaming liquid.

What troubled him? Elizabeth wanted to help if only he would let her.

Reaching over the table, she smoothed over the grooves with her fingers.

His eyes met hers. A flash of green.

The tips of her fingers burned with the intimacy of her gesture. She pulled them back, clasping her hands together in her lap. It had seemed so natural. As natural as William's embrace at the dress shop. It almost made Elizabeth forget she had been forced to marry him three days before. Had it only been three days? It felt like a lifetime ago.

William cleared his throat and straightened his posture away from her. "I have to call at my solicitor's office. I will be away most of the day, but the footmen are at your disposal should you wish to go to the shops."

She tried to hide her disappointment. And she tried to understand why she felt disappointed.

Taking a sip of her sweet coffee, she said, "As exciting as it is to plan a new wardrobe, I have had my fill of it. But since I am free and unoccupied, then I shall follow my heart's desire and spend all day at the bookshop. If I am not home in time for dinner, you may send someone to fetch me at Hatchards."

Elizabeth needed to surround herself with her oldest and truest friends. She had been in town for three days now and had not met one person she knew. Even her letters to Aunt Gardiner had gone unanswered. Elizabeth knew her aunt must be away with Uncle on one of their trips, but it did not lessen her loneliness.

William did not object, nor did he offer to accompany her. "Do you wish for me to inform Mrs. Fischer of your change of plans?" he asked.

The lady's maid interviews. How could she forget? Feeling as if the wind had been taken out of her sails, Elizabeth said, "I will return in time, though the temptation to linger at Hatchards is great."

"The proprietor is well-known to me. I will send

a message to instruct him to charge your purchases to my account. It is yours now, too."

Elizabeth's heart pitter pattered. Books, glorious books! Did William understand what he offered her? She asked, "How many may I purchase?"

William started. "As many as you want, of course."

All the novels she had been waiting for at the circulating library suddenly became acquirable, and Elizabeth could practically feel the weight of the volumes in her arms. She could have kissed her husband! (She did not, of course. But she wanted to. Any man who provided an endless supply of books was worth a kiss.)

First, a gorgeous green gown. Now, as many books as she wanted. Ought she be more cautious? Was he trying to distract her from the truth she sought with gifts?

Would this distrust never stop? Elizabeth hated the constant, uncertain wavering.

No sooner had rational thought put Elizabeth on her guard, than William said, "You will love the library at Pemberley. I wish I could go with you, but I really must see Mr. Rochester today."

Now, that was better. He would miss her. And, he liked books. And, he had a library. That had to mean something.

Was it silly of her to place so much importance on his attitude toward literature? Try as she might to think otherwise, it was important to her. It meant they had something in common.

A WOMAN who would rather spend the day surrounded by books than at the dress shops? Darcy could not believe his good fortune. No wonder Elizabeth's conversation was so well-informed and thought-provoking. He had enjoyed her company the day before as they had gone to the shops Madame Givenchy had sent them to. He would have liked to accompany her to Hatchards, too. But if he wished to leave for Pemberley in four days' time, he had to visit Mr. Rochester that same day. Elizabeth would be safe. They had not seen Wickham, and Darcy would send his largest footman along for protection.

Darcy's forehead still tingled where she had smoothed his brow. A calm he had not felt since he had last held Little Anne in his arms had settled over him. She was not angry with him anymore.

Sleep still evaded him, but for the first time in months, Darcy dared to hope all would turn out well. If he and Elizabeth could continue amicably, they might grow to love each other. An heir would naturally come, and Anne would be safe. Wickham would not want her.

Elizabeth's innocent expression of sheer delight remained in Darcy's mind all the way to Mr. Rochester's office. He would do everything in his power to limit the time of their meeting. He would join Elizabeth at Hatchards. And he would tell her everything that afternoon. It was time.

CHAPTER 18

*P*iccadilly bustled with clip clopping hooves, squeaking cart wheels, and hawkers selling everything from ribbons to eel pies. It was a far cry from Longbourn. The excitement should have cheered Elizabeth. It had the day before.

She had hoped that the anticipation of going to Hatchards would cure her melancholy. Instead, it reminded her of her father.

Elizabeth, twelve years old the last time she had accompanied her father to town, had curled up in a chair with a beautiful tome of painted illustrations while he had spent hours pulling books from shelves, petting their covers, and flipping through pages in an effort to select a few new treasures to add to his own collection at Longbourn. He had spent more than he had intended, but the enchantment of the shop had remained with Elizabeth. She prayed they would work their charm on her that day.

The crowded streets made her crave the fields surrounding Longbourn. She peered out of the carriage's window, but though there were a multitude of faces to see, Elizabeth did not know anybody. She missed Meryton, where she knew everyone. How long would it take for her to feel as contended at Pemberley?

The carriage stopped, and Elizabeth alighted. Slowly, savoring every inch, she stepped past the shop windows into the wonder-filled building where she could fall in love, investigate a mystery, or accompany explorers on a fantastic adventure. The bookshop had not lost its charm. Already, she felt better.

The footman proved useful as she wandered down the rows of shelves, the stack of books she acquired growing quicker than he could accommodate them in his arms. One would think she was royalty with the way he followed her, his eyes constantly sweeping the room as he loomed nearby.

He did not complain under his burden, but common sense told Elizabeth that the pile of books he carried had to be dreadfully heavy after an hour had passed. She was now at the back of the shop, having perused the tomes covering the length of the wall. With another side of the shop yet to delve into, Elizabeth took pity on the footman. "Please take those to the shopkeeper. I will take the five on the top with me to Darcy House, but I think it best for the rest to be wrapped."

The man's eyes widened at "the rest," but he was trained well and said nothing.

Elizabeth, however, could not help adding, "Or perhaps I ought to see about them packing a crate to deliver directly to Pemberley. Mr. Darcy's carriage is grand, but I would hate to have to choose between my books and the trunks containing my new wardrobe." Who was she trying to fool? The books would win that contest without much of a struggle. So long as the green gown made it into her trunk. Everything else could come later.

After securing the area around Elizabeth once again, the footman said, "I will return shortly," and left reluctantly.

William's instructions must have been explicit and concise. While Elizabeth appreciated his concern, she failed to see the danger with which he had clearly impressed the vigilant footman. The chance of her seeing Mr. Wickham a second time was limited. A gentleman such as he would be more likely to frequent the linen-drapers and haber-dashers than a place to improve the mind.

No sooner had Elizabeth turned back to the shelf, than someone behind her began whispering.

"Mrs. Darcy," a man repeated several times, until Elizabeth prayed an attendant would see the tiresome interloper out of doors where he might speak as loudly as he wished.

That is, until she remembered *she* was Mrs. Darcy.

Spinning around, she saw Mr. Wickham crouched at the end of the shelf closest to her.

Elizabeth was instantly annoyed at her own blunder and his furtive manner. She had questions, but her instincts warned he would not give a truthful answer. She said, "We have not been introduced."

Mr. Wickham bowed deeply. "Pray excuse my delight in meeting the woman who has captured Darcy's heart. I suspected you were his wife when I saw how closely you sat in the carriage, and my suspicion was confirmed when I saw the livery of the footman accompanying you. It is an honor to meet you, madam."

"The pleasure is all yours, sir," she said dismissively.

He grinned. "I apologize, Mrs. Darcy, but I could

not rightly approach you with that giant guard dog around."

"You fear his bite, as well you should, when you ought not approach me at all."

Mr. Wickham clutched his heart dramatically. "Your tongue is a sword, madam, but I mean no harm."

"Then why did you wait until the footman left before approaching? Why not call at Darcy House and offer your congratulations like a respectable gentleman?"

He stood a little taller, looking warily in the direction of the front counter. "I am not a fighter."

"No, but from what I gather, you are a great many other things."

His smile melted, and he rubbed his chest as if it ached. "I cannot blame Darcy. There are times I despise myself." Mr. Wickham looked off in the distance, blinking hard and shaking Elizabeth's firm opinion of him ever so slightly. His remorse, whatever the cause of it, seemed genuine.

Without more facts, Elizabeth had no way of knowing how best to proceed. Was this not the opportunity she had wished for? Or should she heed her instinct and William's warning?

Cautiously, Elizabeth asked, "Why are you here?"

Mr. Wickham bowed his head, his shoulders

slumped. "I wish to make peace; to beg for forgiveness. What happened … would I could turn back time…" he stopped, shoving his hand through his hair and shifting his weight.

Just when his conversation was getting interesting. In the hope he would continue without any more help from her, Elizabeth said, "Like it or not, the past is beyond your control to alter."

If Mr. Wickham was an actor, he was an accomplished one worthy of the best stage. Pounding his fist against his chest, he said, "You cannot understand my agony. Not only did I lose my beloved wife, but I lost my brother."

Elizabeth's pulse raced, but she kept her composure. "Brother?" she asked indifferently. As if she did not hang onto his every word.

"Darcy and I were raised as close as brothers, as I am sure you are aware. Mr. Darcy, God rest his soul, loved me like a son — more even — for his kindness to me was borne of want and not obligation. I am not surprised Darcy has not told you of his father's preference. He always was jealous of me."

Had Mr. Wickham's manners been anything but heartbreaking, Elizabeth would have dismissed his crazy words immediately. But it was clear he believed them … and she herself had experienced how fickle the love of a father could be. She held her tongue, not wishing to encourage Mr. Wickham's faulty reasoning.

He stepped closer to her, his palms open. "Please, Mrs. Darcy, I never would have believed it possible for Darcy to marry while still in mourning. Yours must be an extraordinary love for him to act in a manner he would otherwise consider improper."

Elizabeth rolled her eyes, and it was only when she noticed how intently Mr. Wickham watched her that she realized her mistake. The self-satisfied smirk lifting the corner of his mouth proved her reaction had told him something meaningful.

"Not all is well at Darcy House, I take it?" he said. "I wonder, if not for love, why would Darcy marry an unknown maiden from the country? Do not look surprised, Mrs. Darcy. Anything can be found out if one knows the right people." There was nothing in Mr. Wickham's countenance to inspire pity now, and Elizabeth could have kicked herself for her error.

Lifting her chin, Elizabeth said, "You misunderstand me completely, Mr. Wickham. I only found it humorous that you, of all people, should speak of propriety in relation to my husband. He is a gentleman to his bones, and I will not hear you disparage his character." She did not know all of Mr. Wickham's offenses, but she must have hit the mark.

His cheeks blazed; his eyes were lumps of coal in beds of smoking ash.

He stood to his full height, straightening his waistcoat and glaring at her.

Elizabeth regretted not paying closer heed to William's warning. She glanced over her shoulder, hoping to see the large footman approaching.

Mr. Wickham was too smart to hang around any longer. "Darcy would never marry for anything less than the deepest love, and yet, I know your union was made in haste."

"You do not believe in love at first sight, Mr. Wickham?" she retorted.

"No. And neither does Darcy. If you knew him at all, you would know that too."

"Perhaps you do not know him so well as you claim." Elizabeth held her head high, having nothing but the strength of her bluff.

Mr. Wickham narrowed his eyes. "You are helping Darcy hide something, and I mean to find out what it is."

With the agility of a serpent, he slipped away.

It took a great deal of self-possession to carry on perusing the bookshelves as she had before, but Elizabeth felt it imperative for her to act unaffected. Mr. Wickham might be watching, and she did not want to add any more fuel to his fodder. She had added enough already.

Try as she might to disregard Mr. Wickham's comments, one question remained with her.

What was William hiding? Even worse, what complication had she just thrown into their lives?

CHAPTER 19

*H*atchards' charm could not compete against the sense of foreboding Mr. Wickham had provoked in Elizabeth.

To make matters worse, the footman was certain he would lose his place, insisting he did not deserve to continue in Darcy's employ when he had failed so miserably.

Elizabeth had to talk to William. She needed answers.

Cutting short her outing, she returned to Darcy House only to find that William was still out.

Oh bother. Elizabeth instructed the footman to continue as normal until she summoned him. She failed to see how the man could be held accountable for what had happened. Mr. Wickham would have sought opportunity to speak to her until he found it. If not at the bookshop, then perhaps, at a worse time.

Left to her own devices and needing to busy herself in a task which would occupy her mind, Elizabeth wrote another lengthy letter to Aunt Gardiner. She owed her favorite aunt a more thorough explanation after the missive of gloom and doom she had sent the week before her wedding, as well as the desperate plea for her to reply as soon as she and William had arrived in town.

Elizabeth penned several pages wherein she detailed every hope and every fear she held. Aunt Gardiner would understand. That she was away with Uncle, Elizabeth was certain. Otherwise, she and Uncle Gardiner would have traveled to Longbourn to talk some sense into Father before the wedding ceremony. Alas, they had not stormed the church before the service.

Sealing the packet of papers, Elizabeth set it on the corner of William's desk where he also had some correspondence waiting to be sent. She glanced over the names on the envelopes, but nothing stood out as out of place. Not one label saying: In which contains all of Fitzwilliam Darcy's secrets.

With nothing else to do but wait for William to

return, Elizabeth set out to explore her new abode. Mrs. Fischer had given her a tour upon their arrival, but Elizabeth wished to take her time and get a feel for the house. Some residences held a foreboding gloom; others, a peaceful contentment. Longbourn had felt happy to Elizabeth for most of her life. It was how she chose to remember her childhood home.

How would the halls of Darcy House feel? And Pemberley?

Walking down the quiet corridors, she was saddened at the emptiness of it. It felt lonely. Or maybe that was just herself.

A wall of portraits offered some insight. William favored his father, with his dark, wavy hair and strong chin. Mr. Darcy looked fierce, posed as he was with his leg propped up on the chimney and two hounds sitting in front of him. There was a glint in his eye, though, which suggested a sense of humor — whether it was his own or the artist's interpretation, Elizabeth could not discern. He looked solid, decisive, responsible. Just like William. If the portrait was an accurate glimpse into Mr. Darcy's character, Elizabeth could not see him preferring another young man over his own son as Mr. Wickham had suggested.

Unless William told her, Elizabeth would never

know if Mr. Wickham's claims were true or a figment of a disillusioned man's wild imagination.

Lady Anne's ethereal beauty would have drawn a crowd had her likeness been featured in an exhibition. She held young William in her arms, her pose relaxed as she caressed her son. William leaned into her, a small smile curling his lips and his eyes closed. He must have loved her dearly.

They looked so happy. What had happened?

Rubbing some warmth into her arms, Elizabeth turned her attention away from the portraits to the rooms.

The next door was not locked, but it squeaked on its hinges so loudly, Elizabeth looked up and down the hall to make certain she had not disturbed anyone. She had the uneasy feeling that were she to be seen entering that particular room, Mrs. Fischer would sooner steer her away from it.

The thrill of finding a forbidden room was too great to pass after days of frustrated, suppressed curiosity.

Elizabeth stepped inside, closing the door behind her.

Picking her way carefully across the floor, her eyes adjusting to the dim light peeking around the thick curtains, Elizabeth parted the velvet panels.

They were William's favorite color. Blue. Elizabeth looked down at the ring on her finger. It was the same light hue, like the sky on a cloudless summer day.

Had this been Lady Anne's bedchamber?

The room was ready for use. Not one sheet was in sight to cover the polished rosewood desk or the mahogany bedposts holding up a gauzy blue canopy. No, this was not the resting place of a mature matron but of a whimsical girl.

Evelyn had said that William had a sister. Could this be her room? Why did no one speak of her? Common sense told her Mr. Wickham had something to do with the mystery, but she could not imagine how William would permit a man like Mr. Wickham to marry his sister. He would sooner drive him away.

Elizabeth turned to close the curtains lest the bedchamber's occupant should find her there, but something gave her pause. She looked at the fireplace behind her.

There had been no fire in the grate for some time. The bedchamber was cold. Cold and unused.

A dressing table with a silver hairbrush and mirror lay ready for a maid to brush her lady's hair. Several little bottles of perfume dotted the top.

Elizabeth picked up a bottle. Not one speck of dust lingered on her fingertips. Strange.

The room was ready for its mistress, but it was clear the mistress had not set foot in her bedchamber for a long time. Who else resided at Darcy House?

Setting down the bottle, Elizabeth stopped when two bright blue eyes rimmed with dark eyelashes and wheat-gold hair beckoned to her from a round frame. She was a younger image of Lady Anne. She had to be William's sister. Her eyes were wide and innocent, her smile genuine and soft. She looked like an angel.

Why did William not speak of her?

The sound of footsteps jolted Elizabeth into action. Running over to the curtains, she drew them before slipping out of Miss Darcy's empty bedchamber — the feeling that she had stumbled across something she had not been meant to see chasing Elizabeth all the way back to her own rooms.

INTERVIEWING lady's maids proved to be a much more complicated task than Elizabeth had supposed. Most of them were as proud as the ladies they hoped to attend, and Elizabeth could not see herself trusting such a maid (much less confiding in her.)

Evelyn, on the other hand, made up for her clumsiness with her cheerful demeanor and knowledge of the Darcys.

Few things calmed Elizabeth more than having her hair brushed, and Evelyn had a gentle hand despite her claims.

"What can you tell me of Miss Darcy?" Elizabeth asked.

Once again, Evelyn hesitated. Cautiously, she said, "Such a tragic story, hers is. Mr. Darcy has not told you much of his sister?"

Elizabeth shook her head.

"Well, I should not wonder," Evelyn said through a sigh. "Not only was he Miss Darcy's brother, but he was her guardian. If you ask me, he blames himself for her death, although there was nothing he could have done to prevent it."

"Death?" Elizabeth whispered, quite taken aback that she had not read the signs correctly. They were all there. William's unexplainable melancholy, the readied bedchamber she had seen earlier that day, the way none of the servants spoke about Miss Darcy....

Evelyn nodded gravely.

"What happened?" Elizabeth asked.

The brush paused, and Evelyn's eyes met Elizabeth's in the mirror. "He has not told you?"

Elizabeth sighed. Lack of communication was becoming a common theme in her relationship with William. Fitzwilliam. No, William. She could not be angry with him when he mourned his sister. She said, "I know so little. Ours was a brief courtship." Nonexistent, in fact, but Elizabeth would not reveal as much.

Smiling, Evelyn resumed brushing. "Love at first sight! It is romantic. I always thought that if Mr. Darcy did marry, it would only be for the truest, deepest love."

Elizabeth held her peace. She had sworn not to marry for anything less. And yet, here she was.

"I suppose it would not hurt for me to tell you what I know," Evelyn said softly, as if she feared being overheard.

Elizabeth sat up straighter, fighting the bone-melting sensation of the brush in her hair.

Evelyn began, "Miss Darcy married a young man, the son of Mr. Darcy's steward and his own godson. Mr. Wickham."

Elizabeth bit her lips. Wickham. No wonder she had felt William's muscles flinch under her fingers in the carriage. He must have been livid to see his sister's widower with another woman. It made Elizabeth sick to her stomach.

Evelyn continued, her strokes with the brush

slowing, "He is the type of man who is never content, if you ask me. The more he is given, the more he craves. Mr. Darcy's father was generous to him, and instead of being grateful for his kindness, Mr. Wickham gave himself airs. He believed himself deserving of everything he was given and more. Oh, but he is charming! And handsome. Such a waste, if you ask me. Mrs. Fischer says he is as scheming as the original serpent."

William's warning came to mind. It made more sense now. Would he had told her sooner! She would have refused any conversation with Mr. Wickham at all!

Elizabeth imagined Miss Darcy's large, blue eyes smiling in innocent curiosity at the gentleman. "Miss Darcy fell in love with him," she said under her breath, the heartbreaking outcome to such a maiden falling under the spell of a scheming, greedy man who would have used her for his own gain making her nauseated stomach churn. What an awful man!

"Eloped to Gretna Green, they did," Evelyn said so sadly, Elizabeth looked up at the maid's reflection in the mirror in time to see her wipe away a tear before she added, "Broke Mr. Darcy's heart. He did what he could, but the damage was done. Miss

Darcy — that is how all of us remember her … from happier times — showed up at Pemberley months later, alone and horribly ill. She died of consumption about six months after."

Consumption. Elizabeth's eyes prickled. Of all things, consumption. She hated the illness. She hated how it tore families apart. Why had William said nothing of this to her? She could have helped him. They might have brought each other comfort.

Evelyn continued, and Elizabeth breathed slower so she could hear. "Mr. Wickham never called at Pemberley to see her. Not that he would have been admitted, but, if you ask me, any wife would wish for her husband to exert himself on her behalf. She would have liked for him to try, I think."

Elizabeth closed her eyes and groaned. It all made sense now. "The black opal William wears is for his sister," she mumbled.

"Most likely. His father died six years ago, and his dear mother died at childbirth. Lady Anne's last gift to the world was Miss Darcy … and now, she is gone, too."

Elizabeth clutched her stomach. So much death. So much heartbreak. She tried to imagine how William felt as he watched his family disappear one by one, leaving him alone. The last Darcy.

Had loneliness driven William to marry? Was his guilt for his inability to protect his sister from the harsh consequences of her own choices so great, he had jumped at the first opportunity to assist a lady in distress? (Well, not quite distress. Elizabeth would never call her situation desperate until she had exhausted every alternative. But William would have a different view, influenced by his sister's tragic end.)

Most ladies dreamed of a knight in shining armor to sweep her off her feet and ride into the sunset on his white steed. But unlike Lady Gwendolyn with Sir Knightly, Elizabeth wanted her own horse. She did not want her husband to believe her helpless, completely dependent on him for her happiness.

She chewed on her lip while Evelyn continued brushing, chattering about the latest gossip circulating downstairs. It had nothing to do with William or his family, and so Elizabeth was free to ponder her new theories. While it was tempting to think of William as the hero for all that the explanation credited him with a noble motive, it still seemed lacking.

Something was not quite right.

Elizabeth could not justify where she fitted in, and it troubled her.

Evelyn pinned her hair up in a simple bun, it being the extent of her present knowledge of hair arranging, but one she assured Elizabeth she was striving to improve.

A quarter of an hour later, not one hair had escaped from its pin despite Elizabeth's increasingly agitated pacing in her bedchamber.

CHAPTER 20

*D*arcy's meeting with Mr. Rochester had been as brief as he could make it. And still, it took all day. He did not want to miss joining Elizabeth at the bookshop, but he had promised to provide for her, and there were certain details Darcy had to arrange with his solicitor before continuing to Pemberley.

He checked the time. It was late, but perhaps Elizabeth had lost track of the hour as he so often did when he was surrounded by books. Hatchards was not far. It was worth a try. They could go for ices at Gunter's, then in the carriage on the way home, he would tell her about Anne. He burned to tell her. He had waited too long already.

A girl selling flowers on the street outside the shop convinced him to buy a sprig of violets. It was silly, really, but when Darcy saw how the girl had wrapped the stems in a green satin ribbon, he had to buy them for Elizabeth.

With flowers in hand, Darcy entered the book-shop ... to find she had already gone. He was too late.

He looked at the violets and prayed they would not get crushed before he reached Darcy House. Already, the delicate blooms wilted around the edges, though he took care to hold the bunch by the ribbon.

The usual excess of carriages crowding the streets delayed Darcy's return to his residence, and while he did his best to be gentle, the blooms fared poorly. They drooped so badly by the time he reached his house, Darcy did not have the heart to give them to his wife. He handed them to Mrs. Fischer, who appeared red-faced in the entrance hall.

The housekeeper hardly noticed, so marked was her upset. She dropped the flowers into her apron pocket, saying breathlessly, "Something happened. Mrs. Darcy came home early. She spent some time in her rooms before interviewing the maids, then she called Evelyn, the housemaid I have put at her disposal, to her room. Mrs. Darcy has been asking her questions about your family."

Darcy tensed. While few of the servants knew about Anne, all of them knew more about Georgiana and Wickham than he had told Elizabeth. "What did she tell Elizabeth?"

Mrs. Fischer wrung her hands in her apron. The poor flowers were done. "She told her that Miss Darcy died of consumption after a brief marriage to Mr. Wickham. Not much more than that, I can assure you. Evelyn assumes, like everyone else, that your wife is privy to everything that has happened in your household — an assumption I allowed her to continue to believe. Her loyalty to your family is firm, so when I inquired on your behalf, she related the conversation to me in its entirety. I did not think the conversation harming in any way, but I had to change my opinion when I saw Mrs. Darcy in the hall an hour ago. She was out of sorts."

"Out of sorts?"

Pinching her lips and flaring her nostrils, Mrs. Fischer propped her fists on her hips. "She is angry. And from what I gather, she is angry at you. Who can blame her when she has to hear about the family she married into from the maid when her own husband ought to have told her?"

Darcy squeezed his eyes shut and massaged his temples. "Where is she?" he asked.

"Wearing a path in the carpet in your study."

Darcy took to the stairs, alternately lamenting his hesitancy to confide in Elizabeth and her impatient curiosity with each step. He had no right to be cross with her, but he *had* meant to tell her that day.

Unfortunately, intentions counted for absolutely nothing. Would that he had spoken sooner! He knew his disadvantage. He was entering a battlefield on low ground.

Stopping in front of the door, Darcy braced himself and stepped inside.

The air stirred around Elizabeth like a storm. Her eyes were bright, her cheeks in high color. She looked behind him and waved for the footman standing in the hall to enter the room. Darcy had not seen him.

The footman — the same he had sent to the bookshop with Elizabeth — would not look up from the floor.

The muscles around Darcy's neck knotted. He crossed the room to his desk, leaning against it to better observe his wife and the abject footman. "What happened?" he asked.

Charging over to him, Elizabeth said, "Your footman is under the impression you would act unjustly toward him. He insists he will lose his position when all he did was what I bid."

The footman looked up then, and Darcy

observed the effort with which the young man lowered his shoulders and met his master's eyes. "Mr. Wickham was there, Mr. Darcy. I swear on my life I did not see him, or I never would have departed from Mrs. Darcy's side. Not even for a moment."

Darcy's heart pounded in his ears. This was worse than he had thought.

Again, Elizabeth insisted, "He ought not to be punished for what was beyond his control. Mr. Wickham was there, but he hid himself so cleverly, nobody could have known of his presence."

Darcy pressed his eyes closed and massaged his temples. "What did he say?"

"I will tell you everything, but please reassure this young man that his position is secured." Elizabeth crossed her arms over her chest.

Lord, she was stubborn. How could she demand such a thing when Darcy had not yet judged whether her request was reasonable or not?

He crossed his arms, mirroring her stance. He could be stubborn, too. And he had the advantage of rational thought on his side. He was the master of his household. He knew them far better than Elizabeth did. She would not win this argument. "You would undermine my authority in the household my family has maintained for generations in front of a servant?"

She leaned forward, meeting his eyes directly and lifting her chin. "You would turn my concern for one in your household into an attack against your character? You dare assign me such a destructive motive when we have not been wed a week? You know nothing of me."

Darcy felt he did not know her at all at that moment. Looking past her, he told the footman, "We will discuss the matter later. Close the door behind you."

Thus dismissed, the footman left Darcy to face the furious female alone.

Elizabeth eyed him warily, her nostrils flared and her arms still in front of her. "If you are going to strike me, you could at least have the decency to leave the door open. Why hide?"

"What?" Had Darcy not already been leaning against his desk, he would have stumbled back.

Her arms loosened and her glare wavered. "You are not given to a violent temper?"

He was tempted to do something to release his growing vexation, but he would not lay a finger on Elizabeth. Especially now! "No! I have never struck a woman in my life, nor do I intend to start."

"Oh."

That was it? She had accused him of one of the worst evils and all she had to say was *oh*! And this aside from her earlier accusations of drunkenness and immorality. Did she think him a monster? He was nothing like Wickham!

Crossing her arms again, she said, "What am I supposed to think when you do everything possible to avoid answering my questions? You do not speak of your family. You say nothing about your reasons for marrying, and yet I have heard others claim you would never marry for anything but love. Yes, you heard that right. I have been reduced to asking questions of the servants behind your back and sneaking around the house to learn what I can from the unoccupied rooms. I do not understand why I am here, and if you have any kindness at all for me, you would explain why you had to marry, why you chose me, and how we plan to make the best of this mess we are in ... which I must add has been entirely of your creation. Leave it to my father to stick me with the most complicated man in Christendom, and I hate how you can be both maddening and intriguing. I wish I could dislike you completely, but I find I cannot."

Darcy tightened his arms over his chest to keep from strangling his bride ... and from laughing.

Elizabeth was honest, he would give her that. And tenacious. And, right now, he wanted to wrap his arms around her and hold her until she felt safe with him. He wanted to give her reasons to like him.

Blast! How did she do it? Seconds before, she had put him at his wit's end, and now... He wanted to believe her, but he had known the manipulations of others. He could not give in.

Still, it was to Elizabeth's favor that she felt as he did. Once again, circumstances revealed another point they held in common. Trust had to be won, and neither of them trusted the other fully. How could they? Trust took time. Time they did not have.

She accused him of being complicated. He could say the same of her.

Drained of all indignation, Darcy took Elizabeth by the elbow and led her to the couch. The fire had been lit. Leave it to Mrs. Fischer to ensure a more comfortable environment in which his wife could stew.

Taking a deep breath, he said, "You are intelligent, and I will not insult you by implying I do not have another motive for hastening into marriage as I did. I do not wish to be difficult or secretive. I hate secrets."

"And yet, you have so many of them," she said bluntly.

"By necessity."

"You do not trust me."

"As you clearly do not yet trust me, or else why would you believe me capable of striking you?"

Elizabeth wrinkled her nose. "Fair enough, though I have to wonder why you made an offer for me when you have secrets worth hiding. What I wish to understand is where I fit in. Why me? What do you want from me?"

Darcy sorted the facts he could reveal and those which had best remain concealed. Elizabeth was intelligent, and he did not doubt her ability to discern the truth with one slip up from him ... or anyone else. What else had she learned from the servants? What had Wickham said?

As if she had the ability to read Darcy's mind — and, thus, disconcert him further — she said, "Very well. Curiosity and a lack of patience have always been flaws of mine, and I see that you are bent on instilling me with the qualities. You say you hate secrets, Fitzwilliam, and so I will speak plainly. I have no secrets. You have had the advantage of inquiring about me of my friends and observing me with my family. I think that was what you were doing at the Meryton Assembly, were you not? I could not fathom why you would ask about my relatives in Derbyshire when they are in trade or service, or why you should inquire if I liked children. But I have learned enough about you to know you do not make decisions lightly or act on whims. You knew what you were up to, and I played right into your hand. You have used me badly."

Used her? The resemblance of her words to those in Mrs. Reynolds' letter made Darcy's mouth go dry.

Elizabeth continued, "You clearly have the advantage over me, but while I will lay my complaints bare, I must be fair. You are honest … that is, when you deem to speak. If you were to offer a reasonable explanation, I would be inclined to believe you. It is my inclination to make the most of adversity, to soften life's dark moments with humor and the often stubborn hope that with enough determination, I can turn any difficulty into a challenge over which I will come out the victor. Unless you prove unworthy, I aim to win your trust. Your respect. Your love. I cannot settle for less."

Darcy's silence was justified, but she made him feel like a brute. He was not the villain in this story. That was Wickham. She had nearly made him forget.

"What did Wickham say?" Darcy asked.

"He suspects you married to cover over something you are hiding. He told me he means to discover what it is."

Darcy dropped his head into his hands. No, no, no. This could not be. If anything happened to that precious babe…. He pressed the opal against his chest, the clasp cutting against his skin. Darcy's heart lodged in his throat, making it difficult to breathe.

He felt Elizabeth's hand touch his shoulder, smelled the lavender in her hair.

He jerked away.

"William, please talk to me. Let me help you."

"You have helped quite enough already."

"If only you had told me—"

"I told you to stay away from him. I told you he was dangerous, only you did not listen." If Elizabeth had put Anne in danger, Darcy would never forgive her.

Elizabeth pinched her lips closed.

"Tell me everything that happened," he said coolly.

CHAPTER 21

*N*othing worked. Elizabeth had blamed Fitzwilliam's reticence on her own bitter display before, but she had gone out of her way to control her frustration, and he still would not talk.

She meticulously relayed every detail of her trip to Hatchards. She took pride that she did a thorough job of it lest Fitzwilliam find something to disapprove of again. The man was so stubborn! Why did he constantly refuse her? Did he believe her incapable of being of any assistance?

Then again, he *had* told her that Mr. Wickham was dangerous, to stay away. But she had been curious. What else was she supposed to do when her own husband did not trust her enough to offer any explanation? She had married him, had she not? Did that not merit more trust?

Elizabeth poured on the details, talking enough for both of them and hoping some of her excess would rub off on Fitzwilliam.

When she finally reached the end of her narration, wherein she described Mr. Wickham's serpent-like departure, William tugged his hand through his hair and folded his arms over his chest. He was upset. At her. Again. She simply could not win.

Were she more dramatic, she would have thrown her hands toward the heavens and sighed loudly in exasperation. But she was done with dramatics. She crossed her arms and held her breath.

Fitzwilliam inhaled, his lips open to speak, and Elizabeth braced herself, already preparing several quick retorts. She would accept some of the blame for not heeding his warning, but not all of the fault was hers, and she would make certain (nicely) that he knew it.

"He never would have approached you had I been there, and for that I apologize," William said.

Elizabeth blinked. "What?" Another apology? She raised her hand before he repeated the words again. "No, I heard. It is just that I was expecting a reproof."

"You were armed for battle, were you?"

She did rather feel like a battered warrior. "Well … yes."

William considered her. "If love is a battlefield, you are headstrong enough to win."

Taking courage in his compliment (she hoped it was a compliment), she advanced. "As are you. Unless we join forces, we waste precious energy we could better use to fight your secret foe."

His golden green eyes moved over her face. Elizabeth did not know what William searched for, but she prayed he would find it in her. How could they ever get along if they did not take a leap of faith and trust each other?

She regretted her earlier remark. William would never hurt her intentionally. He was far too responsible. Only, she had felt so angry, so frustrated, so trapped.

"What have you found out about me and my family?" he asked.

Elizabeth tried to contain her groan. Her and her big mouth. Not only was the footman in danger of losing his position because of her, but she had now put Evelyn at risk. It would not take much effort for William to discern her main source of information. And, she did not fail to notice how smoothly he had changed the subject.

"Mostly good things," she said, purposely vague.

"Such as?"

He would find out sooner or later anyway, and as disgusted as Elizabeth was with secrets, she became more determined than ever to keep nothing from him. She would be an open book. "I learned that your mother and father were a lovely couple. I should have liked to have known them."

William swallowed hard, looking away from her to the flickering flames in the fireplace. "What else?" he asked.

She spoke softly. The topic was clearly a painful one. "I learned how gentle and elegant Lady Anne was; how all the ladies mimicked her gowns. Your father loved her deeply. It was difficult for him when she died, but his attachment to your sister was strong enough to keep him going."

William nodded, his gaze still fixed on the fire, unblinking. "And so it was. He lived for my mother. When she was gone, a part of him died along with her."

Elizabeth could not imagine anything more romantic — to live for another. She craved such a love. But the sadness in William's voice forced her to see how such a union, torn apart by death, had affected their son.

Reaching over, she placed her hand on top of his. "You loved them dearly, too. I am sorry," she said.

He blinked, looking down at their hands. For a moment, Elizabeth considered pulling her hand away. But he did not flinch, and so she did not move either. His warmth was comforting.

He asked, "What did you learn about my sister?"

"That she was as lovely as your mother." Elizabeth bit her lips together, dreading that he should ask for more. Which, of course, he did. There was an urgency about him that overcame her reluctance.

She continued, "She married Mr. Wickham, and then she returned to the one safe place she knew — to you — when she fell ill with consumption. She died months later."

"Three months ago next Sunday," he whispered.

Elizabeth's heart stilled. "What?" She shook her head, not wanting William to have to repeat himself when her question was prompted by disbelief, not poor hearing. "So soon?"

He fiddled with the opal in his cravat again. He was in mourning for his sister. He had married while he was in mourning.

While gentlemen were known to carry on with their lives much sooner than society allowed women to after a death in the close family, Elizabeth sensed that William's grief had not yet dulled. His emotions were fresh and raw. Had his need to marry been spurred by an emptiness he could not fill? If that was the case, why did he not let her close? Would he ever let her into his heart?

"Why did you marry me?" she asked. She needed to know.

He turned his hand over, squeezing her fingers against his palm. His jaw clenched, and she could see the battle engaged in his mind. He did not want to tell her, but Elizabeth trusted he would. Otherwise, why the struggle?

She bit her tongue and held her breath, trying not to lose her patience as she had before.

She waited. And waited.

Finally, he spoke. "When I asked you if you liked children…" he started.

Elizabeth could have filled his sentence in a dozen ways — *…it is because I run an orphanage. I have an abundance of nieces and nephews I adore. I love children and want a family of my own. I have a child of my own. I am a widower. My mistress left me a child…* — before he finally did.

"…it is because I have a child at Pemberley. A child nobody, not even the servants here, know about."

A secret child. Elizabeth did not want to believe it. William had kept a mistress.

"You married me to cover an indiscretion?" she asked, to be certain.

"Yes."

Disappointment washed over Elizabeth, but she refused to let it carry her away. She focused on the silver lining, blurred as it was by tears she would not shed for a man she could never bring herself to love completely. It was all she had. She had read too many novels and scandal sheets to be ignorant of the habits of most gentlemen with the means to indulge their fancies. She never should have assumed her husband was any different.

Shoving the woe-is-me dramatics from her mind, Elizabeth doggedly concentrated on the good.

Good … good … what was good? It was not so easy to find, but Elizabeth stuck with it. If not for William's sake, but for her own. And the baby's.

The baby.

What kind of a man raised his mistress' offspring? Honor. Yes, that was a very good quality. Most gentlemen cast their unwanted children off, leaving the poor innocents without a protector or a helper in the world. William's honor in caring for his illegitimate child was worthy of a degree of respect. He was responsible.

Responsible. That was good. Another excellent trait. It was not a quality Elizabeth was accustomed to observing in her own home. Perhaps that was its appeal. It calmed the bile churning in her stomach and loosened the knot in her throat (at least it had until she thought about it.)

She had to think of the child.

Whatever William's faults, Elizabeth did not have it in her to punish an innocent child for his or her father's poor choices. She knew all too well what that felt like, and she could not be the cause of it.

Taking a deep breath, she met William's eyes. "Why are we tarrying in London, then, when we ought to return to the child? Am I correct to assume the baby resides at Pemberley?"

His sigh was so profound, it sounded like a cry. Lifting her hand to his lips, he kissed her fingers and pressed her palm against his cheek. Short whiskers chaffed her skin.

It was a small victory, and she had not won without injury, but Elizabeth knew she had gained a foothold in William's confidence. The big question was: What would she do with his trust if she could not forgive him? Did she even want to fight for his love now that she knew his whole heart was not his to give?

CHAPTER 22

*D*arcy's admiration for his wife increased a hundredfold. Already, she put Anne's needs before her own, foregoing her green gown so that they might make haste to Pemberley.

Madame Givenchy made her displeasure known, threatening to travel to Pemberley with Elizabeth's wardrobe herself to oversee the final fittings. Darcy offered to send his carriage for her if that was what she was determined to do, but he would not stay another day in London now that his wife insisted they leave.

While Madame Givenchy deemed it unforgivable for him to allow his bride to travel in the gowns she had brought from Hertfordshire, Elizabeth made hasty business of finding a lady's maid to suit her — a girl already in his employ and with whom she had developed a degree of friendship. The very maid who had proved to be Elizabeth's greatest source of information. At least, Evelyn was loyal. She would not speak against Darcy or his family. More importantly, she would not be a danger to Anne.

He was on his way home to Anne. Three days with decent weather and frequent horse changes, and he would hold her until he could not feel his arms.

And thus, the day following their conversation in the drawing room, he and Elizabeth began the journey north to Pemberley with no more luggage than they had carried with them to London (excepting, of course, a small box of books from Hatchards.)

Elizabeth was quiet for most of the trip. She often directed her gaze out of the window. At first, Darcy supposed she was simply taking in the scenery. She had mentioned how she wished to know more of England. He knew how much she enjoyed being out of doors. But one could only look at dirty roads, bare tree branches, and fallow fields for so long.

Occasionally, she spared a weak smile for him. But only her maid could provoke Elizabeth to speak more than a sentence at a time.

Darcy supposed she merely needed more time to

adjust to his revelation; to the knowledge she would be a mother. He, too, had much to ponder and plan.

Three uneventful days of arduous travel later, the carriage turned off the main road to the widened path that would lead them to Pemberley. To Anne. Darcy leaned against the side of the carriage, pressing his fingers against the glass, willing the coachman to drive faster.

"Is this Pemberley?" Elizabeth asked.

He nodded.

She slid closer to the window, and Darcy sat back to allow her a better view.

Her lips parted, and she said in awe, "It is beautiful. I can hardly believe I am to live here." She looked at him, and Darcy watched her smile fade when their eyes met. It was hardly the reaction he had hoped for. Was this the same woman who had proclaimed she would never back down from a verbal altercation? The same woman who demanded answers? Darcy had groaned at her relentless curiosity many times, but now, he found that he missed her spirit. The Elizabeth who sat across from him was much more cautious and guarded. More like himself.

He ought to have been thrilled.

Mrs. Reynolds pinched her lips in displeasure when she met them at the carriage. He had not heeded her advice to stay on in London.

The housekeeper, however, was all smiles and welcomes to Elizabeth, herding her away from Darcy's side to introduce her to the servants she had lined up to receive them.

Elizabeth charmed them all when she repeated their names, making an effort to learn who they were when most ladies did not concern themselves with the identities of their servants so long as the work was done. His mother would have approved of his choice. She would have liked Elizabeth. *He* liked Elizabeth. He liked her very much.

Seeing how well she fitted in at Pemberley infused Darcy with hope. All would be well. They were home. He could protect Anne. And he admired his wife. Love would come. It had to.

Mrs. Reynolds had a spread ready for them in the parlor. The fire had been lit in anticipation of their arrival, and the warm yellow walls felt like rays of sunshine. It was a cheerful room, and Darcy thanked Mrs. Reynolds for her thoughtfulness. He could use some cheer, and he was certain Elizabeth could too. He ached to see Anne, but he did not quite know how to proceed. He could not leave Elizabeth alone.

Before Elizabeth could pour the tea, she stepped closely to Darcy. Looking about carefully, she rose to her tiptoes and whispered in his ear, "I wish to see the baby, if you please."

This was the moment he had been anticipating … and dreading.

He hesitated.

Elizabeth's silence during their journey had allowed space for worry. What if she resented Anne? What if she did not understand his need to protect her — to honor the promise he had made to Georgiana?

He would not get the answers he craved any sooner by tarrying. Darcy held out his arm. Without a word, he led her up the stairs and down the hall to the room beside his bedchamber.

It was quiet. Was Anne sleeping? He would suffer Mrs. Bamber's censure and wake her. He had been away too long — long enough to fear Anne might not remember him.

Mrs. Bamber was lifting Anne up from the cradle when Darcy opened the door and stepped aside to allow Elizabeth to pass. The curtains were open, and Anne was alert and cooing.

Darcy's heart leapt at the sight of her, and as nervous as he was to show her to Elizabeth, he could not prevent the smile from spreading over his face. How he had missed his little girl.

Elizabeth did not wait until he had introduced the nurse to cross the floor. Darcy hastily made introductions.

"Mrs. Bamber? That was my aunt's unmarried surname," Elizabeth said, fingering the pink blanket. "I thank you for caring for the child while William was away. May I hold her please?"

Darcy widened his stance by the door and crossed his empty arms over his chest, reminding himself that this was exactly how he had dreamed Elizabeth would react. He would just have to wait his turn.

Cheeks pink with pleasure, Mrs. Bamber lowered Anne so that Elizabeth could see her better, holding the baby out for her to take. Anne's big eyes were bluer than Darcy remembered them being. A tiny tuft of golden hair that had not been there when he had left for Hertfordshire curled over her forehead.

He had been gone too long. Had Anne forgotten him?

Elizabeth gasped. Eagerly cradling Anne against the crook of her neck, Elizabeth exclaimed, "She is your sister's!"

Darcy was tired of not knowing what to say, but he was truly and completely flummoxed. To whom else was the baby supposed to belong? "Yes. Anne is the reason I had to marry. I have to protect her."

Clutching Anne closer, Elizabeth swayed and twirled, clearly overjoyed. "You are the beloved niece, not the secret daughter! Oh, but you are darling. You are the image of your mama's likeness. She was a beauty, as was her mother before her. And you are too! Oh, I am so happy, I could burst!"

Darcy's ears rang. Secret daughter? Had he heard her correctly?

Mrs. Bamber clapped and laughed. "You chose well, Mr. Darcy. Madeline has a special place in her heart for Miss … er, Mrs. Elizabeth."

Darcy could not have answered had he tried, nor could he comprehend his wife's glee when she had been silent for the past three days.

Elizabeth spun to face the nurse. "You are the one who recommended me to William? Based on my aunt's opinion?"

"I did. Mrs. Reynolds and I would do anything to see Mr. Darcy happy and Baby Anne secure." Mrs. Bamber touched Anne's blanket. "I have been this wee one's nurse since the day she was born. Not just any lady would do, you see? And Madeline is everything sensible. She would never speak so well of you unless you were deserving of her praise."

The women chattered happily, leaving Darcy to stew by the door, his annoyance only tempered by the tenderness with which Elizabeth held Anne. It was as if Elizabeth had always been at Pemberley. As if she had always belonged. As if Darcy was not in the room at all.

Anne rubbed her face into Elizabeth's neck and chirped contentedly. Had she even seen him? Surely, she would have reached for him if she had. He had not been gone so long, he was now a stranger, had he?

Stepping closer, all Darcy's concerns were appeased when Anne pounded her little fist against Elizabeth's arm and cooed directly at him. Now, that was more like it. The other females could forget him, but not his Little Anne.

With a kiss on Anne's cheek, Elizabeth handed the baby over to him. "Your *uncle* William," she said.

Of course, he was her uncle. What else was he supposed to be … oh…. Of course. Darcy froze as full realization dawned. "Who did you think Anne was?"

Elizabeth blushed, and her voice was quiet. Tenderly covering over Anne's ears, she whispered, "I thought — and with just reason, might I add — that she was your illegitimate child."

Secret child. Yes, he had heard her correctly.

"How could you think such a thing?" Darcy said a bit forcefully.

Patting Anne on the back, Elizabeth shushed him. "You are startling the baby, Fitzwilliam."

Oh, so *he* was in trouble now? Because she

errantly thought he had fathered an illegitimate child?

Elizabeth reached for Anne, but Darcy jutted his chin toward Mrs. Bamber. If he had to release the sweet child to anyone, it would be to the more reasonable woman in the room.

His arms freed, Darcy crossed them over his chest.

But his wife was every bit as annoyed at him as he was at her. He saw it plainly in her face with her flared nostrils and bunched eyebrows. Clutching her wadded fists at her hips, she said, "What else was I supposed to think, Fitzwilliam, when you would not tell me your secret? I spent the entire journey from London fretting that my father had forced me to marry a man whom I could never truly love and respect when you are everything honorable and good and wonderful."

He could not win with this woman. "That makes you angry?"

"Why should it not when we have wasted precious time? All the worry and concern—"

Mrs. Bamber tried to excuse herself, but Elizabeth stopped her. "Do not leave. Not when I am guessing you are the one responsible for putting ideas into Fitzwilliam's head."

As if he had not made the choice himself! Darcy's

anger renewed at Elizabeth's accusation and her repeated use of "Fitzwilliam."

Redirecting her ire to him, she continued, "Yes, that makes me angry. You made me distrust you with all of your secrets when you could have simply told me the truth."

Darcy ground his teeth. He had never lost his temper at the fairer sex, and he would not allow his wife to provoke him to shout now. *I did not yet trust you*, he grumbled in his own mind as he took a deep breath.

"We have wasted valuable time — time we should have used working together to protect this sweet child," Elizabeth said, her voice softening as she gazed again at Anne.

Another deep breath. Elizabeth's tenderness toward Anne — a baby she had only just met and to whom she had no connection outside of her unwanted union to him — was a wet blanket over Darcy's ire. Calmly, he said, "I did not know how to tell you. She means the world to me, and I did not know how you would receive her. I would do anything to keep her safe."

"How could I be anything but supportive when your every action since I met you at the assembly has been moved by your intense love for the babe? She was the reason for your haste; why you wished to depart for Pemberley so soon. Had you told me, I would have understood. You only needed to trust me to help you." She pushed his chest with her finger. "All that talk about being unaffected by emotion…" She grinned, adding, "You cannot know how relieved I am to see proof contrary to your claims."

She stepped closer to him, and Darcy knew he ought to retreat. But his stubborn feet remained firmly rooted in place.

His pulse galloped as she drew closer still, until her toes touched his and he could feel the warmth of her nearness and smell the lavender in her hair and wonder what on earth she was talking about.

He shook his head. Now that she knew about Anne, she had to know all of the truth. Darcy hated to alter the coy glint in her eyes and the impish grin gracing her plump lips, but neither did he wish for Elizabeth to believe a lie.

"My motive was not so altruistic as you think. I married you to keep a promise. It is my duty, my responsibility, and my honor to protect my sister's child. I would rather die than fail her."

Elizabeth looked over her shoulder at Mrs. Bamber. "Sounds like love to me, do you not agree, Mrs. Bamber?"

Mrs. Bamber pinched her lips together and fussed with Anne's blanket. She said nothing, but the smile she attempted to conceal was reply enough. At least, Elizabeth seemed to think so.

"See? Mrs. Bamber agrees with me, and I think I know how much you trust in her opinion if our union is any indication…"

Darcy did not like the ease with which Elizabeth stole his former ally away from him. Nor did he appreciate how fickle his reasoning sounded coming from her mouth. He had yet to tell her of his need for an heir. She would not think so kindly of him once he told her. And he would tell her. As soon as there was a pause in the conversation.

Mrs. Bamber smiled at Elizabeth. "You are exactly as Madeline described you. She will be happy you are here."

"She will?" Elizabeth turned away from Darcy to face the nurse.

"Of course. I did not say anything to her before, not thinking you would return to Pemberley so soon after marrying, but she will be delighted Mr. Darcy chose you. Mind you, Madeline knows nothing of the babe, nor can she. You cannot breathe a word to her no matter how tempting it might be."

Darcy waited for one of the ladies to take a breath so that he might get a word in, but their ability to speak as quickly as they did without air was amazing.

Elizabeth said, "We left London before I could say anything at all to her. More is the pity. I could use her advice right now."

"Well, then, have Mr. Darcy send a messenger to the inn to fetch her."

Darcy blinked. The infamous Aunt Gardiner was here? In Derbyshire?

CHAPTER 23

*W*ho was Sir Knightly compared to her husband?

Just remembering the look on William's face as he held Anne was enough to make Elizabeth's heart gush. She had understood his struggle then — when his immense love for the infant was plain to see. The tenderness with which he caressed his cherished niece....

Elizabeth fanned her face. If he could love her like that, she would be very happy indeed.

They had been married one week. They had known each other a fortnight. Until then, she had considered her marriage a forced one. Not anymore. William had called it a marriage of convenience, but she could not agree with that either.

She wondered how they would remember their story ten years from now.

Lady Gwendolyn could keep her Sir Knightly. Elizabeth had William.

To her immense pleasure, he sent for her aunt and uncle immediately.

After they learned of their niece's quick entry into matrimony, and had recovered from their shock, they were thrilled to be shown the house before dinner. William did not relegate the task to Mrs. Reynolds. He showed them himself, and Elizabeth watched him speak of his family's estate with as much love and reverence as he did of the people who had once graced Pemberley's halls. The void they had left in their absence was great, but it was nothing Elizabeth would not attempt to fill.

Aunt Gardiner shared what stories she could of William's family and their servants (whom she knew more intimately.)

When they neared the hall of portraits, Aunt Gardiner paused in front of Lady Anne's likeness, saying "A true lady, and a memorable beauty." Turning to William, she added, "I was so sorry when she died. It must have been difficult for everyone, but I will never forget how my father described Mr. Darcy at her funeral."

William looked up at his mother's portrait. "She

was dearly loved by all. I believe most of the villagers surrounding Pemberley came. It was kind of Mr. Bamber to come."

Aunt Gardiner inclined her neck, looking at William. "Especially was she loved by the husband and son she left behind with her newborn daughter. My father was there when Mr. Darcy broke down and wept. He saw how you stayed at his side, holding him up when grief dropped him to his knees. You were only a lad of twelve years, but you acted beyond your age. Not once did he recall seeing you cry. You were too busy seeing after others."

William was silent. He spun the opal in his cravat between his fingers, the only sign he gave of his struggle to maintain his composure.

Elizabeth slipped her hand into his, delighting in the way he spread his fingers to make room for hers.

Uncle noticed. He smiled at Elizabeth, then, with a meaningful look at Aunt, he cleared his throat and said, "Yes, well, it would appear that a crooked path has been made straight and all will turn out well in the end. That is not always the case, and I am over-joyed to see evidence of our Lizzy's happiness with a gentleman who thus far appears deserving of her." He leveled his gaze at William.

"I do not think I could ever truly deserve her, but

I will always try," William replied, gently squeezing her hand.

Elizabeth was more determined than ever to prove her worth. She would never allow him to consider casting her off.

The butler came to announce dinner. Flickering candles and sparkling crystal chandeliers lent a lightness to the grand room, and soon, the conversation turned to livelier topics.

Uncle Gardiner regaled them with stories of their travels, and Aunt Gardiner complemented his accounts with details he would have overlooked but which added to the telling. They finished each other's sentences, and several times their eyes met as they silently shared a memory which Aunt did not repeat aloud. Elizabeth longed for a union like theirs.

William laughed several times — a smooth, rich baritone she would like to hear more often.

Elizabeth suspected she knew how she fitted into William's life now, whether he recognized it or not. He would say he needed a mother for Anne — to love and protect the child as her own. And Elizabeth accepted the responsibility, understanding the honor in being bestowed such a trust. She would give her heart freely to the babe. Already, she planned the adventures they could have exploring Pemberley together.

But Elizabeth was confident in her new role, and it had little to do with the baby. William needed her. He needed her cheer, her laughter, her love. She only had to help him see it. He had shouldered the burdens of others alone for so long, it would not be easy for him to allow her to ease some of the weight from him.

William so rarely spoke about his sister, Elizabeth snapped to attention when he said, "Georgiana would have liked to hear what you have related about our mother."

Aunt pushed her dessert plate away, setting her napkin on top of the table. "There is something I must say now that I have the opportunity. It has plagued my conscience ever since I learned Miss Darcy got involved with Mr. Wickham."

Elizabeth's pulse slowed.

William's voice dropped. "Yes?"

Twisting her hands together, Aunt barreled on as quickly as she could speak, pausing only for the quickest breath. "As you know, my father sold everything from boot polish to ribbons and buckles in his shop. Several times, he extended credit to Mr. Wickham, and several times he had to appeal to Mr. Wickham's father to cover his son's debts. Had it not been for your father's generosity, I am certain we would have been forced to sever all business ties with the Wickhams. I remember how Mr. Wickham would walk through the store, fingering all the items displayed on the shelves as if he owned them and had every right to take what he pleased. A couple of times, he did."

"He stole?" Elizabeth gasped.

"He did not see it as stealing. He believed he had a right to whatever he pleased." Directing her words at William, Aunt continued, "I knew this about his character — his sense of entitlement — and yet I said nothing. I knew how kind your father had been to him, and I did not wish to offend Mr. Darcy. However, there was one conversation I overheard which particularly disturbed me. It happened shortly after Lady Anne's death. Mr. Wickham came into the shop, and my father asked him to please settle his bill. I do not remember every word, but I remember how it ended and the feeling of foreboding which has plagued me ever since. He said that he was practically a Darcy, that with Lady Anne's death (of which he did not speak with enough delicacy to suit me or my father), he was the second son Mr. Darcy would never have. He spoke of Pemberley as if he had some claim on it."

Elizabeth shuddered, but she was not surprised.

In her brief interlude with Mr. Wickham, she had been given a similar impression.

Aunt Gardiner reached for her wine glass. Taking a sip, she continued. "I met Edward around then, and he convinced my father to return to London with us when we married. With so many changes, I will own that I gave little thought to the conversation I had witnessed. But when I heard of Miss Darcy's elopement with Mr. Wickham, I felt guilty for not warning you before departing from Lambton. Had I said something, perhaps she might have seen his true character. Or perhaps you would have known to exercise greater caution around him. The truth is, I never considered it possible for him to manipulate himself into your family."

That was the exact reason Elizabeth had not connected Georgiana with Mr. Wickham sooner. She had not imagined it possible.

Aunt's voice shook. "I am so sorry. I trusted my reason instead of intuition, and I wish I had acted differently. I wish I had trusted you enough to do as you saw fit."

Elizabeth clutched the fabric near her throat. Trust. It all came back to trust.

William did not speak for some time, but when he did, his voice was firm. "Thank you, Mrs. Gardiner. Allow me to reassure you that I was not ignorant of Wickham's deceit. It is I who must bear the burden of guilt for permitting him to comfort my sister after our father's death. I had thought of him as a brotherly figure for so long, it was easy to assume Georgiana saw him in the same light. Pray trouble yourself no longer over this affair."

He blamed himself for his sister's disastrous choices. No doubt, he blamed himself for her death too.

Elizabeth's compassion stirred, and while the conversation had revealed Mr. Wickham's ugly motive, it had also taught her a great deal more about her own husband. She owed her aunt a hearty embrace.

Uncle Gardiner summed up the matter nicely. "Communication, even when it is unflattering and painful, is vital to establish trust and maintain healthy relationships. It is why our trade flourishes and why our union is a happy one, and it is what I most wish for our dear Lizzy with you, Mr. Darcy." Raising his glass, he toasted their health and happiness.

Elizabeth drank to that.

CHAPTER 24

*D*arcy had enjoyed the dinner party with the Gardiners. His connection to Elizabeth aside, he gladly would have sought out their friendship. Their cheer, their protective nature toward Elizabeth, and their positive outlook inspired confidence and offered a brief respite from the fear and anxiety gnawing at him. He ended the evening more at ease than he was accustomed to.

Elizabeth, also, had seemed more relaxed in their presence. Her humor shone, and the dining room echoed with their laughter many times during the course of the meal.

It reminded Darcy of the meals he had enjoyed with his family in his youth. Pemberley had been a peaceful, happy place then. Would it ever return to its former glory? Darcy had seen glimpses of it that night. It was enough to make him believe it possible again, though he dared not allow his hope to get the better of him. Not until he was certain.

Mr. Gardiner's advice echoed in Darcy's mind. Communication. Trust. His own father had extolled the value of trustworthy friends, and Darcy knew from experience how important open communication was in the smooth running of a household. Unfortunately, trusting others was not so easy after suffering the betrayal of those closest to you. Emotion had blinded him, clouding his better judgment. The greatest betrayals stemmed from misplaced trust, and Darcy was cautious. Perhaps, overly cautious. He ought to have trusted Elizabeth more from the start. He ought to have trusted his instincts about her.

Not lost on him had been Mrs. Gardiner's admission of conscience for not acting on her better instincts — on emotion. She had apologized to him, and while he had not thought it necessary, he had appreciated the kindness in her disclosure.

He had apologized to Elizabeth more over the last week than he could recall apologizing to anyone else in his lifetime (or so it felt.) Darcy wished to break that cycle by avoiding the mistakes he had made to provoke the need to make amends in the first place. But, where to start? He had kept too many secrets for so long, it did not come easily to speak at all let alone confide in the woman who would bear the burden of his trust with him.

When he thought of Anne and her needs, Darcy easily justified his actions. He could not have done anything else.

By contrast, when he thought of how those same actions affected Elizabeth, Darcy felt like a selfish creature. He ought to have confided in her. Several times, he had considered telling her, but the voice of reason had raised valid doubts.

He needed more proof of her trustworthiness.

He needed more time.

He was not yet ready.

So many excuses. It became impossible to sleep.

Chased by an uneasy conscience, Darcy tucked his shirt into his breeches and went to his study. The growlery was cold and dark, and Elizabeth was not there. Not that he expected her to be at that ungodly hour.

That same logic did not appease his disappointment when he went down to the library. She was not curled up on a chair with a book in her hands.

Peeking into Anne's room, half expecting to find Elizabeth swaying the baby in her arms, Darcy again was frustrated. No Elizabeth.

This was foolish. She would be asleep in her

bedchamber as he ought to be. As a normal person in possession of their senses would be.

Darcy paused in front of Elizabeth's door in the hall. Was it his imagination, or did he see the flicker of a candle under the frame?

Not trusting his eyes, he pressed his ear against the door. Was that a rustle he heard?

Stepping back, Darcy pondered his next move. He ought to return to his bedchamber, but sleep would not come until he talked to her. Elizabeth needed to know the truth. All of it. And he needed to tell her while his determination was strong.

Holding his breath, he tapped lightly on her door.

There. If she was as restless as he was, she would answer. If she was asleep, his tap was too light to disturb her slumber.

Thump.

Darcy leaned forward. Had he really heard a thump or had he imagined it? It was impossible to hear anything at all over the drumming of his heart.

He stood thus for what felt like forever. The door did not open, nor did he hear any other sounds to inspire the hope that it would.

Exhaling his breath, Darcy turned down the hall, resigning himself to another sleepless night.

The creak of the door swinging open abruptly on its hinges startled Darcy so much, he jumped.

Elizabeth's white nightgown glowed in the light of the fireplace. She looked fierce, the fire's flames reflecting off her hair and casting shadows around her illuminated figure. Darcy's mouth went dry, and his pulse galloped, the thin linen of her nightgown revealing the soft lines and rounded features from which he could not tear his sight. Not even the hat pin Elizabeth wielded over her head like a dagger pointed at him frightened Darcy to sanity.

A battle of his heart and mind ensued. Elizabeth was his wife. Was it not his privilege to gaze upon her, to appreciate her as a husband should? Surely, there was no harm in merely looking.

He groaned. Who was he fooling?

Darcy slapped his hand over his eyes, but the image was burned in his mind. "I am sorry. I did not think…" his words trailed off. That was precisely the problem. He had not been thinking. What did he expect but to find his wife wearing a nightgown in her own bedchamber at this hour of the night? So much for acting on impulses.

"I do not mean to stab your eyes out, Fitzwilliam. Put your hand down." Elizabeth sounded annoyed.

Lowering his hand, Darcy fixed his eyes to the floor.

"It had occurred to me that your reason for marrying so quickly might be to produce an heir, and until I am convinced otherwise or we fall in love, I will not allow my husband to treat me like a broodmare. To think I had almost put the pin away after tonight's dinner," she scolded.

Good Heavens! Darcy felt a blush spread over his entire body. Of course, she would assume he had come to claim his husbandly privilege. "That is the last thing on my mind, I assure you." (Well, it *had* been until he had seen her in her nightdress. That much was true.)

"Oh." She lowered the hat pin. "Well, why are you here, then?"

Now, she sounded disappointed. Would he never understand her?

Darcy looked up at her, trying to keep his gaze focused on her face. Trying, and failing repeatedly.

"Do you not have a wrap or a shawl?" he grumbled.

She looked down, her eyes widening when she saw the display. Crossing her arms and legs over herself, she spun away from him. "Have you no decency? Close your eyes!" she exclaimed.

Her snappish tone riled him, and he answered in turn. "I am not the one lacking decency, and may I point out that I covered my eyes as soon as you answered the door until you told me — quite crossly — to put my hand down?"

The ridiculousness of their situation hit him, and Darcy swallowed hard to conceal a chuckle. He swallowed hard again when he looked up just before Elizabeth wrapped herself in a blanket. She had a marvelous backside.

He shook his head, feeling guilty when she spun back around to face him. Guilty for appreciating his own wife. Was there such a thing as too much irony?

Making sure he was watching her, Elizabeth made a point of returning the hat pin under her pillow. The gleam in her eye as she spoke belied her usual humor. "Now you know my secret. I sleep with a hat pin under my pillow to ward off my husband's unwanted advances."

Offended to the core, Darcy said, "I would never make advances unless you wanted them."

She lifted her chin. "And I would not want your advances unless you wished to give them."

Communication. This was not communication. This was bickering, and while they seemed to have a talent for it, arguing would lead nowhere.

Taking a settling breath, Darcy said, "My reason in coming was to lay bare everything I have been unable to tell."

"Unable or unwilling?" she asked.

The question could have carried a harsh bite, but

she seemed too interested in his reply to have already passed a judgment.

Her eagerness to understand made it more difficult to answer. He could not confide Georgiana's history with just anyone — not even his closest friends and most certainly not his relatives.

Unable.

But, while Elizabeth might receive that reply with more compassion, it was not the whole truth. It disowned him of all accountability for his role, yes, but it also made him a powerless victim. And that, Darcy was not.

Unwilling.

"I do not like secrets, William."

At least, she was not calling him Fitzwilliam. Yet.

He did as she would do and used humor to diffuse the gravity of the conversation to come. Maybe, it would make the words easier to utter. "Is that why you hid a hat pin under your pillow?" he teased.

She smiled. "A weapon is only as good as its hiding place."

"And a secret is only as safe as the confidante in whom it is entrusted."

Elizabeth nodded, her smile fading. "When I saw your sister's baby, I understood your silence." She lifted a finger. "Mind you, she cannot justify you completely. You still ought to have taken the time to see if you trusted me *before* we married, and once our names were signed in the wedding register, you should have included me. However, I will be lenient for the baby's sake."

Her ability to lighten the air in the room was awe-inspiring. "Thank you."

She went over to the settee by the fireplace, waving for him to join her.

He closed the door behind him.

Sitting beside her, careful to keep a proper distance between them, Darcy asked the question that had been bothering him since their arrival. "What made you think Anne was my illegitimate child?"

"You said you had a child — a secret child. You had also admitted to having your heart broken. Since you did not explain from whence the child proceeded, I had to suppose it was from you. After all, I had been told that your sister died of consumption. It never occurred to me that she might have had a child."

"She died in childbirth just as my mother did."

"I am sorry."

Darcy exhaled. "Me too. She would have liked you." As soon as he said it, he knew it to be true. Elizabeth would have been a good friend to Georgiana. He rubbed his chest, the pressure rising to his throat so great, he thought it would crush him. He had come here to speak, and now he could not.

Elizabeth slid closer to him, her hand touching his. How perfectly her fingers had fitted between his. Darcy would not mind it at all if she placed her hand in his once again as she had done earlier in the hall, but he did not feel free to initiate the gesture with what he had to tell her. The truth was, he had meant to use her. He was little better than Wickham.

She said, "If you are anything like your mother or your sister, I think I would have liked them very much too."

Darcy scoffed. "I am not worthy of your admiration."

"You took care of her until the end. What is not to admire in that?"

"I failed her. It was my responsibility to keep Georgie safe, and now she is gone."

"You could not have known what she would do or how it would end. You did the best you could. You are caring for her child as tenderly as if she were your own."

Why did Elizabeth insist on defending him? He did not deserve her good opinion. "My big plan was to protect Anne by providing an heir of my own, but I am a selfish wretch who was so blinded by duty I failed, once again, to consider the interests of the woman who would be my wife. No, Elizabeth, do not speak kindly to me." The words poured forth from Darcy like water bursting out of a water lock.

"So, it is true. You married for an heir."

"You were right to doubt me."

She rested her head against his shoulder. "While I have concealed a hat pin under my pillow, I have not seen fit to use it, though we have been married a week. Had you been the brute you seem to think you are, I would have stabbed you by now."

He exhaled, her forgiveness overwhelming him when he had done so little to merit her understanding. "I do not doubt it. I would have deserved it. You could not have wished for this."

She sat upright, facing him, commanding his full attention. "You know nothing of my wishes, and you are hardly in a position to tell me what to think, so I insist you stop trying. I will be the judge of my own opinions regarding your character."

Opinions? She had more than one? Darcy determined it best not to ask.

Elizabeth, however, was eager to tell. "Despite the many opportunities I have had to think ill of you, you have proved to be honorable and responsible. I do think that, perhaps, you take your responsibilities a bit too seriously, but since it involves a defenseless child whom you love more dearly than you will own, I can hardly fault you that. That is what I think of you, William, and it is what I will continue to think until you prove otherwise to me."

She would discover his faults soon enough, but it was balm to Darcy's soul to know Elizabeth thought well of him just then. She was the only person in the room who did.

Darcy wished more than anything to hold that moment, to preserve it. But he had learned long ago that good things are not meant to last. Time was treacherous like that. It tore families apart in the most painful way. It stole what should have lasted forever. It had turned him into a liar.

Resting his hand over hers, needing the strength of her touch, he said, "Then it is time I told you what really happened, of the lies I have told to hold what is left of my family together."

CHAPTER 25

*E*lizabeth clutched William's hand, leaning into him and offering him what support she could.

Slowly, as if he were reliving the details as he narrated them, he began, "I allowed Georgiana to set up residence in Ramsgate in the summer of her fifteenth year. She loved the coast, and we had many friends there. It was her first opportunity to run a household, and she reveled in it. I saw it as good preparation for the time when she would marry and have her own family. My cousin Colonel Richard Fitzwilliam, who was her guardian along with me, agreed it was a good plan. Georgiana wrote often, telling me of her learned experiences and successes. I stayed away longer than I would have otherwise, not wanting to impose on her recently acquired freedom. I had not felt her so happy since the death of our father."

Of course, William would see his sister's new opportunity as an exercise in duty and responsibility. He would never understand how such newfound freedom could go to a starry-eyed maiden's head. Elizabeth dreaded to hear the rest, knowing that Georgiana's story had not ended as it should have.

"One day, I got word that she had eloped with Wickham. The companion I had employed had proved to be treacherous and facilitated their union. I did not know he had been courting Georgiana. She had made no mention of him in her letters."

And end her fun by telling on herself to her big brother? Elizabeth thought. Clearly, William was not at all familiar with the romantic notions most females of a certain age held. How could he have known if Georgiana had purposefully kept it from him? Pinching her lips together to keep from interrupting, Elizabeth listened as William continued.

"Wickham calculated his plans well. He knew I was in London at the time, and Richard was away with his regiment. Had I been at Pemberley, had Richard been on leave, we could have intercepted them. As it was, I arrived too late. They had married over the anvil."

To be so close, but too late. William must have

been crushed. He would not have been completely blind to Wickham's faults. He would have known how miserable such a man as Wickham would eventually make the little sister William had been entrusted to protect. Elizabeth wondered if Wickham had given Georgiana any kindness at all once the deed had been done, or if her dreams had shattered the same day as their wedding.

William cleared his throat, his voice tight and forced. "I paid Wickham her dowry — thirty thousand pounds. Without it, Georgiana would have been forced to face the reality of the life she had chosen much sooner. It was my weak attempt at delaying the inevitable. Wickham spent it in months. He wrote to me demanding more just as Georgiana's letters became less frequent. I did not know if Wickham intercepted our letters, but I wrote every week to tell her she was always welcome at Pemberley. That I would always be here if she needed me." The tension in his body spread to Elizabeth, and he gripped her fingers. She held onto him as tightly as he did to her, her heart breaking for him and aching for a girl she had never met; for the daughter Georgiana would not get to raise.

"She came home," he said, his voice trembling.

Elizabeth wiped tears from her eyes. William would not cry — perhaps he never had allowed himself to when everyone looked to him for strength — but sitting as closely as she was to him, Elizabeth felt the weight of his emotion. She would share his challenges. She would help him raise Anne with all the love and affection she possessed. No child should be forced to pay for her parents' mistakes, an opinion Elizabeth had always held but which was felt with much more intensity of late, thanks in whole to her own father.

Her father. Elizabeth did not want to think of her father. It was difficult to think ill of the ill. She would deal with her burdens later. Right now, she would help William with his.

"She must have seen your reassurances and taken comfort in them," she said.

"She slept for five days, too weak and exhausted to say a word. It was Mrs. Reynolds who told me of her condition. We did not know how far along her confinement was, but we persuaded Georgiana to stay until the child was born."

Elizabeth was puzzled. "Persuade?"

"Wickham's hold on her was so great, she would have returned to him. She was convinced he would change for her, that he only needed more time. She blamed herself for falling ill and tiring him."

Elizabeth gasped. Her body burned with anger. What sort of man allowed a young lady barely more than a child herself to bear the blame of his behavior? If Elizabeth had disliked Wickham before, she hated him now. He did not deserve sympathy.

The bitterness in William's tone told her his sympathy had worn out long ago. He continued, "I knew that if Wickham thought he could get more out of Georgiana, he would attempt it. She had nothing left to give, nor was I content to allow her to waste away. Not when I had been entrusted with her protection. So, I told him she had consumption and was too ill to travel. I told him she would have to stay at Pemberley under my care and that of my family's best physicians. I lied."

"As any loving brother ought to have done," Elizabeth defended. How many times could a heart break? She had lost count. How awful it must have been for William to witness. "He never came, did he?" she whispered.

"Not once. Not that I encouraged it. I might have run him through had he attempted to come."

"I would have done the same." She was tempted to carry her hat pin on her person on the chance she saw Wickham.

William relaxed his grip around her hand, a faint smile softening his expression. "I am glad to hear it. Toward the end, I think Georgiana was disappointed enough in him that she would not have returned.

Too many times, I saw her looking out of the windows toward the road. She knew he did not try to come. She knew he did not write, though she asked the butler as soon as the post was delivered every day. The month before Anne was born, she stopped waiting, and it was during that month when she directed all of her energy and attention to her unborn child that I saw the woman my sister would have become." His chin quivered. "Our mother would have been proud. I was."

Elizabeth wrapped her arms around William, her face pressing against the soft linen of his shirt. She felt his labored breathing and held him tighter. Tears were a sweet relief, and she would squeeze them out of him if it lessened his anguish.

Finally, with a deafening rush of air at his lungs, William enveloped her in his arms, bowing his head over hers. He shook silently, his breath coming and going in bursts. Elizabeth's arms tired and her neck cramped, but she did not loosen her grip. William would be there to hold her when her turn came.

She would be as steady for him now as he would be for her. As he had been for his sister; for his father. As he without a doubt was for everyone he loved. He confused duty and responsibility with love, but it was there and it was strong. It also offered the proof Elizabeth needed. William loved her — not with the ardent passion she desired ... yet ... but he loved her enough to forgo his duty in favor of her consideration. How it must have tortured him to spend a week in London for a silly gown when his heart and conscience demanded he return to his beloved niece.

He pulled away from her, wiping his face and distancing himself. "I am sorry. I am not given to displays of emotion."

"More is the pity," Elizabeth sighed. She longed to help ease his burdens, and William seemed intent on bearing them alone.

When he looked at her strangely, she added, "It is normal to grieve the ones we have loved and lost. Our hearts are full of so many sentiments, its only recourse is to shed the bitterness in tears. But what it leaves behind are the pleasant memories. Those, we get to keep. Those are what we treasure, for they allow us to remember our loved ones without grieving their loss."

He blinked at her. "Maybe someday I will know what that feels like. I miss her too much now."

Elizabeth did not know which "her" he meant — his mother or his sister — and she chose not to ask when there was still more to be said. "I understand why you wish to keep Anne away from Wickham, but why must she be a secret? We cannot hide her away forever. It is not good for her to be restricted to her room at Pemberley with so few for company."

William's eyes were dry now as they met hers. He searched her face intently as he spoke. "Until I have an heir of my own, Anne stands to inherit Pemberley, Darcy House, and the entire Darcy fortune. Our estate is not entailed, and she is my closest relation. Anne is the last of my family."

Now, that was taking it a touch too far. Straightening her shoulders, Elizabeth said, "You have me now. We are a family, and I will help you." She meant it. It was a relief to have a foe other than her husband to fight. He was an ally now, and whether he liked it or not, they were a team. All of her bitterness and disappointment now had an appropriate target. She would pick up the battle where Georgiana had left off. Elizabeth would protect Anne … and she would fight tooth and nail against Wickham should he trespass into their lives. He had caused enough damage in the Darcy household. It stopped here.

William's eyes were particularly green, his chin speckled in prickly hairs the same color as his wavy ebony hair. His chin was firm and his arms were solid.

Elizabeth had always believed him handsome, but William's character added to his appeal. She felt herself falling, and while a part of her trusted him to guard her heart, Elizabeth prayed he would not cast her off.

"Before she died, Georgiana made me promise to take care of Anne as my own. She made me swear to keep Wickham away from her, to protect her," he said.

There it was. The little worry that nagged at her. What would William do if he had to choose between fulfilling his vows to her and keeping his promise to his sister? It was a choice she would never ask him to make. That would not be fair. But, what if it happened?

Elizabeth shook the doubt from her mind.

They sat together in silence, their fingers entwined. For now, it had to be enough. All she needed was more time with William. Then, she would be certain of the constancy of his love.

Elizabeth could have stayed on the couch with William forever, but she must have fallen asleep. She woke in her bed, alone, the following morning. The hat pin was still under her pillow.

CHAPTER 26

*W*illiam rubbed his fingers over his lips, remembering how Elizabeth's hair had tickled them when he had kissed the top of her forehead the night before. She had been light in his arms as he had carried her to her bed. He could have spent all night holding her, listening to her steady breathing and watching the changes in her expression as she dreamed, but she deserved to rest after their journey. He also did not wish to startle her and end up with a deserved stab from her rather sharp hat pin.

He slept deeply, feeling more rested the following morning than he had in a very long time.

When he checked on his niece, Mrs. Bamber told him that Anne, also, had slept like an angel all night.

Peace had settled over Pemberley, and William

marveled at Elizabeth's ability to put everyone at ease when she had only just arrived.

The weather turned for the worse, bringing winter upon them with fat drops of incessant rain. Normally, he would have bemoaned the loss of his daily rides, but William reveled in the opportunity the rainclouds gave him to court his wife.

Much of their days were spent in Anne's nursery, where Elizabeth knelt on the floor to encourage Anne to crawl and chattered with her about everything from the scientific explanation for the colors in a rainbow to whimsical stories of talking frogs and toads. She exceeded every hope Darcy had dreamed of in a mother for Anne … and a partner in life for himself.

Mrs. Bamber enjoyed the extra time they allowed her to tend to her own family while, together, they cared for Anne.

Mrs. Reynolds was delighted. With a hand over her heart and tears in her eyes, she said, "It is just like having your mother and father back."

Darcy's respect and admiration grew until he could not imagine his life without Elizabeth, nor did he wish to do so.

Taking Mrs. Fischer's advice, he brought a breakfast tray to Elizabeth every morning, buttering her toast and sitting with her while she ate and they conversed. He prepared her coffee how she liked it, and he took care to leave her bedchamber before he was tempted to incite her to use her hat pin. He would not so much as kiss her as he longed to do until that object was removed from under her pillow.

Every day, Mr. and Mrs. Gardiner joined them. They would picnic in the conservatory and spend hours conversing in the music room. William learned a lot about Elizabeth's childhood during those discussions. It was then, he realized the depth of Mr. Bennet's betrayal. Elizabeth had gone from being his marked favorite whose happiness he had boldly defended to sacrificing her prospects to secure the futures of his wife and other daughters. While Darcy had thought Mr. Bennet's actions to be responsible at the time, he now understood how it had been a harsh blow to Elizabeth. He never wanted her to feel dispensable when she was so important to him.

Dinners were a pleasant affair now. It was during one such dinner, William reached over to touch Elizabeth's hand. "May I ask you a question you may be hesitant to answer?" he asked. He feared her reply, but he had to know.

She smiled. "You may ask anything you wish."

Darcy ignored the nauseating knot twisting in his stomach. "Do you regret marrying me?"

"No," she said without wavering, her quick reply merciful on Darcy's taut nerves as she continued, "My father's actions and your initial distrust aside, I believe that had we met under more favorable circumstances, I still would have accepted your offer to dance. I would have anticipated your calls and enjoyed our conversations. And I am convinced that I would have chosen you had I been given the choice."

"How can you be so certain? We have only been married a fortnight."

She arched an eyebrow. "A fortnight full of trials is better than a year of calm in learning a person's true character. What about you? Do you regret marrying me?"

"Not at all."

"Even when I was argumentative and bitter?"

"Especially then." William did not know how to explain it, but he would try. "Even with the circumstances which led me to hasten to marry, I wanted a wife I could admire, a lady with opinions and views of her own."

"Even when they are contrary to your own?"

William smiled. "Growing up here, with a mother and father who loved each other dearly, I observed how they complemented each other, how they made each other whole. I could not imagine one without the other. And yet, they did not always agree. In fact, given their opposing temperaments, they very often disagreed."

Elizabeth's eyebrows knit together. "But you called your mother elegant and graceful. I had imagined her more … perhaps, complacent?"

"She possessed a strong mind, and my father encouraged it. They debated often — more amiably than you and I have done, but I credit that to a lack of practice."

She chuckled. "We shall improve in time, then? I like that. I really would have liked to have met your mother."

"She would have loved you. As I … have grown to … I mean to say, I rather like…" Darcy was bungling this, but he tried again. "I did not realize how incomplete I was until you came. It is like a miracle has come into my life, and that miracle is you." He shook his head at himself. A poet he would never be.

Elizabeth raised his hand to her lips, brushing them over his fingers. "Oh, William. Sweet words, indeed, but your actions — thankfully — speak much louder than words. Mrs. Reynolds told me she heard from her sister, who told her about the bunch of violets you meant to give me. I would not have cared that they were crushed."

Darcy felt his face warm.

"When we arrived here," Elizabeth continued, "I had a letter from Jane. She told me how you had sent a physician to Longbourn to examine my father. I know the great lengths you have gone to for the security of my family, and I have seen how gentle you are with Anne. There are many more I could mention, but I do not want you to think so much of yourself, you become overly proud; then you would be difficult to live with and I would regret ever saying anything favorable at all," she ended with a twinkle in her eye.

Darcy laughed. "Can I not be proud of my choice in a wife?"

"Of course, you may. It shows your good taste," Elizabeth teased. "You will need to remember that when you have little use for me or tire of my company."

His laughter died. Is that what she thought? That he was no different from her father? "Why would you think that is possible?" he asked.

Clasping her hands in her lap and staring down at them, she said, "Feelings can change over time."

"Mine do not."

"My father loved my mother when he married

her, and now they barely tolerate each other." She chewed her lip, her gaze still fixed on her lap.

"While mine grew in love for each other with every day they spent together. I do not wish to be any other way."

Finally, she looked up, tears sparkling in her eyes. "I used to be my father's favorite. I know he loved me. But he cast me off too easily when it was convenient to him. Did you know that the doctor you sent to Longbourn told him that he did not have consumption?"

"What?" Darcy pulled his chair closer to Elizabeth.

"Jane told me in her letter. My aunt and uncle were shocked when I told them. He had implied that he had been properly diagnosed in his letters to them, so when they made inquiries to other doctors regarding his symptoms and treatment, they were not given any good news."

"What about the blood?"

"It was from a cut in his throat, not his lungs."

Darcy shoved his hand through his hair. "And the coughing?"

"Between the remedies the neighbors brought for him and your doctor's recommendations to quit smoking his pipe, his cough had improved enough for Jane to mention it. I suspect his health has been fully restored by now. I am glad of it, I really am. I only wish things had happened differently." She rubbed her arms, looking small in her chair.

Darcy stood. Extending his hand, he pulled Elizabeth to her feet and wrapped his arms around her. He was not Wickham. Nor was he Mr. Bennet. He was her husband, and he would be what she needed him to be.

She buried her face against his chest, and he tightened his grip around her, resting his cheek on the top of her head.

"I will not break my promise to you, Elizabeth."

"I want so badly to believe it," she whispered against him.

CHAPTER 27

*U*ncle Gardiner pretended to read the paper while Elizabeth conversed with Aunt Gardiner, who listened intently while sipping her tea in the inn's private room. It was another dreary day, but Elizabeth felt like she was full of sunshine and rainbows.

"With such a dreadful beginning, I never dared to dream I could be this happy. This past week has been so perfect, I fear something will come along to spoil it. Or that I will wake up and find it was only a dream."

Forgoing all pretense of reading, Uncle dropped his paper to the table. "You cannot imagine how relieved we are to hear it, Lizzy. When we learned what your father had done, his presumption in assuming the role of a doctor to diagnose his own illness and forcing you to marry the first man to offer, we were enraged."

Aunt patted his hand. "Calm down, my love. That is done now. While Mr. Bennet acted in an unforgivable manner, we must look at the positive and appreciate how well it has turned out for our Lizzy." Squeezing Elizabeth's hand, Aunt said, "We could not be happier for you, dear."

Folding out his paper once again and holding it up to the scant light coming in through the window, Uncle said, "It is a pity Mr. Darcy could not join us today, but flooding fields spare no landowner. He is a good man for seeing to the needs of his tenants."

The fire crackled beside them, and Elizabeth was grateful for the warm room and the good company. She, too, wished William were with them instead of out in the cold rain. She had asked the cook to prepare his favorite meal and for his valet to be ready with hot bathwater on William's return. He had been so attentive to her, she could do no less for him. He had been away most of the day, and already she missed him.

Pouring more tea into their cups, Aunt excused herself. "I shall return shortly to hear more about your dashing Mr. Darcy. Oh, and then maybe you will allow me a turn with the paper. I saw an article about stolen jewels that promises to be entertaining."

Uncle chuckled. "Sometimes the paper is as diverting as a novel."

Elizabeth made a mental note to find and read the article Aunt referred to while Uncle said to her, "With all this rain, it is no wonder the fields are flooding. I daresay others are faring far worse than Darcy's tenants are. He is such a responsible young man and as quick to catch on to new ideas as you, Lizzy. The other day, we discussed the state of current trade, and I was impressed with his insight. He is a good man."

Elizabeth smiled. "So you keep saying. I am happy you have become fast friends. I hope that next time, you will join us with the children at Pemberley." She bit her tongue before she said anything more. They were not free to have guests until Anne was theirs to keep. It was too risky. Oh, but how Anne would love her great cousins.

Aunt returned shortly, much too soon to have done anything more than turn back at the stairs leading up to their rooms. Her eyes were wide and her cheeks pallid.

Elizabeth stood, reaching out to hold her aunt's arm before she swooned. Aunt Gardiner never swooned. What was wrong?

Uncle dashed to her other side, leading her to the

nearest chair. "My dear, what is wrong? You look like you have seen a ghost."

"Not a ghost, my love." Turning to Elizabeth, she said, "I just saw Mr. Wickham. He is here."

It was too late, and Darcy was too exhausted to return to Pemberley that night. Chilled to the bone and covered in mud, he rode to the hunting lodge and staggered inside. He did not bother to light a candle. His muscles ached, and while a bath sounded like the solution to all of his ills, he was too exhausted to heat water. The thought of returning to those same fields on the morrow was enough to make a stronger man groan. His arms felt like lead and his back ached from hours of shoveling. The exertion of prying his boots off his feet was enough to convince Darcy that his best option was to wrap himself up in blankets and succumb to sleep. Morning would come too soon, and if he wanted to finish his work early so he could return home to Elizabeth and Anne, he needed to rest now.

Darcy thought of Elizabeth. Contemplations of her had kept him warm all day, and she was the last image he remembered until he awoke hours later. It was still dark, but that would not stop him. The glow of the moon was enough. He wanted — he needed — to see his family.

ELIZABETH SLEPT POORLY.

Wickham had stayed in the tap room until nightfall, and she could not risk leaving the private room for fear of him seeing her. And so, she had waited. And waited.

Finally, when he retired to his room, she made her escape, returning to Pemberley the way she had come — in her uncle's carriage. How grateful she was that she had accompanied them into the village instead of taking the Darcy carriage. Wickham would have recognized it.

William had not returned, and when Mrs. Reynolds suggested he might have decided to spend the night in the hunter's lodge closer to the fields as he had several years ago with his father, Elizabeth had wasted no time penning two notes. One to be delivered to him directly. Another to be left for him at the lodge should he have already left the fields.

Elizabeth would take no chances. She wished she could have gone herself, but she could not leave Anne. Not with Wickham so close. She had slept in the nursery, checking on Anne every time her dreams woke her, and she had to make certain the baby was safe in her cradle.

It was dreadfully early, but Elizabeth knew she would not be able to rest. Not desiring to wake Evelyn, she donned her morning dress with the fewest amount of buttons and slipped out to the hall.

She peeked into William's room, but his bed had not been slept in.

Continuing downstairs, Elizabeth gasped when she saw Grayson pacing in the entrance hall.

"Have you not slept at all either?" she asked.

"Until Mr. Darcy returns, I do not feel I can."

Worry chased away Elizabeth's exhaustion. "Did he get the notes I sent?" Nothing would keep him away from Anne if he thought her in danger.

Grayson's frown deepened. "The stable boy I sent to the lodge returned to Pemberley last night. He assured me he left the note in the center of the table next to the lamp. If Mr. Darcy lit the lamp, he could not miss it."

Elizabeth nibbled on the inside of her cheek. "And the other messenger?"

"He has not returned."

"What?" She reached out, steadying herself against the nearest wall until Grayson insisted she sit on the chair he had formerly occupied.

"I sent another messenger after him, but the lad could not find him."

Elizabeth clutched her stomach. "Could it be he is a friend of Wickham's? Might he know about Anne and betray us?"

Grayson shook his head. "He did not know the contents of your note. He could not have known what news it bore or how urgent its message was. I fear he has come upon an accident. The weather was stormy, and it was dark when he departed."

While Elizabeth did not wish for any harm to have befallen the rider, she prayed the explanation for his absence was as simple as Grayson suggested. She dropped her elbows to her knees and squeezed her hands against her temples. Should she send another messenger? Ought she wait to see if William saw the message when he woke?

Debating her next move, Elizabeth's heart nearly jumped out of her throat when someone tapped on the entrance door.

Giving her a meaningful look, which told her to stay put, Grayson stretched himself to his full height and opened the door.

"I am sorry, Mr. Grayson. I would have used the service entrance, but I knew you would be pacing the hall here and I wanted to waste no time," a man said hastily.

Elizabeth ran over to join them. It was the messenger.

"Did you deliver the note to Mr. Darcy?" she asked.

The rider doffed his cap and bowed his head. "I am sorry, ma'am. I cut across the forest to reach the fields. It is quicker that way. But the path was slick with mud and it was too dark for me to see. My horse stepped in a hole." He shook his head, twisting the cap between his hands. "I had to choose: Leave the horse suffering and continue on foot to deliver the message to Mr. Darcy or see to the horse, then return here to try again on a fresh mount at daylight. Knowing Mr. Darcy to be a just man, I decided to see to the horse."

Elizabeth wanted to cry, but she kept her composure when the messenger patted his pocket and said, "Your note is safe here. I will deliver it to Mr. Darcy as soon as the sky lightens up enough to see beyond my nose."

She replied as she imagined her husband would. "You did well. How is the horse faring?"

"For a moment, I thought I would have to put the beast down, but he stood. He was lame all the way, and our progress was slow, but we made it back to the stables. The groom will soon have him put to rights."

"Mr. Darcy will be pleased. Now, pray give me the note. You have had a long night and are in need of some rest and warmth. I will ask someone else to deliver it." Elizabeth extended her hand.

The messenger shuffled his feet. "If it is all the same, ma'am, I would rather see the task through. There is time enough for me to dry before the fire before I go again. This time, I will not fail you. I will ride with more care."

"Very well. Thank you."

He left, and Elizabeth sank back into the chair, head in hands. "Can anything else go wrong?" she groaned.

She felt Grayson's presence beside her. In a firm tone that brooked no argument, he said, "You have done what you can. We are all proud to serve you, Mrs. Darcy."

Tears burned Elizabeth's eyes. If she was so much appreciated, why did she still question her value to William? Why did she still doubt? If only she had proof — irrefutable proof that went beyond William's assurances. She did not think him a liar (though he claimed to be one for Anne — Elizabeth would have done the same and did not fault him for it), but she needed evidence before she dared to believe that William was her true love. She needed him to say the words. To prove them beyond her ability to doubt.

She looked up, smiling weakly at Grayson when her throat was too tight to utter thanks.

"Come now, Mrs. Darcy, allow me to show you to the breakfast parlor."

Elizabeth shook her head. She could not possibly eat. "I would like to return to Anne."

Grayson bowed. "I will keep watch here."

"Please send for me as soon as William returns."

He bowed again, and Elizabeth retired to the nursery. Anne cried when she came in, and Elizabeth was glad for the excuse to pick up the baby. Holding her snugly against her, Elizabeth hummed and sang softly until both of them drifted off in slumber.

CHAPTER 28

*R*aised voices startled Elizabeth awake. How long had she been sleeping?

Anne's velvet lashes splayed over her plump, rosy cheeks. She slept soundly still.

Elizabeth removed the blanket over them, looking around the room when it dawned on her that someone must have put it there.

Evelyn darned a stocking while Mrs. Bamber knit by the fire. Stabbing her needles into the ball of wool, the nurse rose from her chair, her arms out to take Anne. "You both looked so peaceful, we did not wish to wake you."

"Someone is here. I hear voices." They must be coming from below the window.

Mrs. Bamber frowned. "I will stay here with the

child. If it is Mr. Wickham, I will steal the child away before I hand her over to the likes of him."

"Is it he?" Elizabeth asked.

"We cannot see from the window, but we suspect it is. Who else would show up shouting at our doorstep before calling hours?"

Elizabeth wiped the sleep from her eyes and gathered her wits. "Is William home yet?"

"Not yet," replied Evelyn. "Are you certain you do not wish to stay here with us?"

"If it is Wickham, and William is not here to toss him off the property, then I shall have to do it for him." Elizabeth rushed down the hall, the voices growing louder as she went.

Grayson, flanked by two large footmen, blocked the door. Elizabeth did not need to see to know it was, indeed, Wickham.

"What is this?" she demanded, silencing all four men as Grayson stood to the side and the footmen moved to either side of Wickham. They were trained well. All three of the men looked ready to pounce at Wickham's slightest move.

Mincing no words, Elizabeth said, "You know you are not welcome here."

Wickham smiled. "Ah, Mrs. Darcy. How glad I am to see you."

"I doubt that. Speak plainly, Mr. Wickham. Why are you here?"

His smile faded. "I came to collect what is mine."

Elizabeth's heart hammered against her ribs. He knew. Her stomach lurched, but she swallowed hard. She would give nothing away. Raising her chin, Elizabeth feigned ignorance and more confidence than she currently possessed. "Who? Your wife? I fear you are rather late for that. Georgiana has already been laid to rest. You can make her suffer no more."

Wickham pointed inside. "She was with child. My child. Darcy has no right to keep my child from me."

Elizabeth forced herself to breathe slowly, continuing her bluff. "A wild notion if ever I heard one."

"You deny it? I saw the scullery maid washing baby linens. You are too recently married to require them, so I made inquiries. I know Darcy is keeping the child from me just to cheat me out of my inheritance."

Drat it all, he knew. She would have a word with the scullery maid, but the damage was done. He knew. Having no recourse but to continue in the same attitude, Elizabeth said, "Do you suppose the elder Mr. Darcy meant to overlook his own natural son from the wife he adored to give Pemberley to you, his godson? You are delusional, Mr. Wickham, and I wish for you to leave at once before I summon the magistrate's constables."

"Mr. Darcy loved *me* like a son! Me!" Wickham pounded his fist against his chest.

At Grayson's nod, the footmen took the intruder by the shoulders, pushing him farther out of the entrance.

Straining against them, Wickham shouted, "You will not get away with it! The child is mine. I will return, and I will take what is mine. You have no claim. I will be back."

Elizabeth clasped her hands in front of her so that he could not see how they shook and ordered him off the property.

Grayson closed the door. The footmen would escort Wickham all the way back to the inn at Lambton if need be.

The butler's silence was heavier than usual, and one look at his gray eyes revealed that Elizabeth's worst fear was justified.

Her whole body quivering, she sat on the chair nearest to the door, determined not to move from there until William crossed the threshold.

"Would you like me to bring you a cup of tea?" Grayson asked.

"That would be just the thing. Thank you, Grayson. Did the messenger deliver the note?"

"He did. He only returned a few minutes ago. He said Mr. Darcy would follow shortly."

"Good," Elizabeth exhaled.

No sooner had the maid set a tea tray down on the table beside Elizabeth than the front door burst open.

William stood dripping wet in the hall, his hair plastered against his head and rain water streaming down his greatcoat to puddle on the marble floor. "I got your note. I saw Wickham leaving under guard. He did not harm you, did he?"

He looked so cold and forlorn, so concerned over her welfare, Elizabeth jumped to her feet. Wrapping her arms around William's waist, she pressed her cheek against his chest and said, "He came for Anne. We did not let him near her."

William's arms crushed around Elizabeth, the rain from his coat seeping through her morning gown. She did not mind in the least. William leaned against her just as much as she supported herself against him. Together, they would face the man who had used Georgiana. Together, they would protect her daughter. Together, they would safeguard their family.

"WHAT DO WE DO?" Elizabeth asked.

Darcy had been pondering the same question as he had listened to his wife relate all she had been forced to do in his absence. He valued her strength of character, quick wit, and protective nature more than he could ever express. Her ability to deliver the news he most dreaded to receive and inspire hope filled him with pride. He loved her. Truly, ardently, unalterably, he loved her.

"Anne is safe because of you," he said, wanting so badly to pull Elizabeth back into his arms, to kiss her soundly.

She left the side of Anne's crib to join him by the fire, extending her hand out to him as she got closer. He took the hand she offered, turning it over to kiss her palm, then the inside of her wrist.

He did not remember how she ended up on his lap — nor did Darcy care so long as she stayed there. He ran his fingers up her neck, her skin smooth, her hair silky. Pulling her closer, he brushed his lips over hers softly, feeling her breath tickle against his skin.

As quickly as she had settled into his lap, Elizabeth stood in front of him, trying to tug him to his feet. "Come, William. Anne might wake, and Mrs.

Bamber could return any moment. We cannot make an heir here."

Her words were an easterly wind snuffing out his ardor. Is that what she thought? That his affection was motivated by a commitment to keep the promise he had made to Georgiana? That he was using her? "I am sorry. I had no right."

"You are my husband. You have every right."

Darcy did not understand her puzzled expression, but he was unwilling for her to doubt the genuineness of his attachment. "Not like this. Not when you think I expect it of you."

"But Anne is not safe until you have an heir. It is why you married."

He could not deny it, though he wished to. How was he supposed to kiss his wife when she would misunderstand his expressions of love as an act of duty? Should he tell her he loved her? Darcy saw the question in her eyes, but if he told her how he felt right then, she would not believe him. She would think he only said what she wanted to hear to get what he needed to protect Anne. When Darcy made love to Elizabeth, he wanted her to be certain it was because he loved her. He did not want the taint her father's betrayal had cast over her or the shade of Wickham's usury to ruin what ought to be a true expression of Darcy's undying devotion to her.

Holding her hands between his, he bent over until their foreheads touched. "If I could relive the past, I would still choose you."

"But Anne—"

"I love Anne more than my own life, and I will fight to keep her, but you are the one with whom I wish to spend the rest of my days. I would no sooner disappoint you than I would endanger her."

"Then, we must not lose her to Wickham. I must give you an heir."

Darcy shared her determination, but the moment had passed. There would be no more kisses for him that night.

CHAPTER 29

*E*lizabeth leaned against the wall on one side of the open door of the antechamber and nodded at Evelyn, who stood opposite. They were ready.

The entire household was on the watch for Wickham. They had known he would call soon.

William had not wanted Elizabeth to be present, not knowing what vitriol the viper would spit, and this was Elizabeth's compromise. While she would have preferred to glare at Wickham directly rather than eavesdrop from a nearby room where they could hear everything without being visible, she did enjoy being the recipient of her husband's protective aspirations.

She brushed her fingers over her lips, recalling how they had tingled under his kiss. So light and tender. A perfect first kiss that had left her wanting more.

William's refusal had been a blow … until she understood that he did not want her to feel forced or used. Uncle was right. William was a good man.

Now, Elizabeth's heart melted a little every time she looked at him. He had not said the words she most needed to hear, but she was confident William would not say them until he truly meant them. Otherwise, he would have said them last night.

And so, there was nothing left to do but wait. She prayed William did not make her wait long.

"They are at the door," Evelyn whispered, leaning as far out of the doorway as she dared without being noticed.

Elizabeth wished she could see. From the upstairs windows overlooking the drive, she had watched Wickham riding with another man. All she had been able to ascertain was what Mrs. Reynolds had told her. With a huff, the housekeeper had said, "Mr. Hanslock is the magistrate. His property runs the length of Pemberley along the north side. He is a harsh man, who sees generosity as a flaw and understanding as a sign of a weak mind. He has a grudge against the Darcys."

Not a promising beginning. Grabbing Evelyn,

Elizabeth had run downstairs to the antechamber before the gentlemen had reached the door.

Wickham's voice shouted, "This man is a kidnapper and a murderer. He took my wife from me, and now, he attempts to hide my offspring out of sheer spite. He has always been jealous of the affection his good father had for me, and this is his way of avenging himself. He is using me for his own gain."

Now that was the pot calling the kettle black. Even Evelyn snorted and rolled her eyes.

A sharp voice spoke. It must be Mr. Hanslock. "Mr. Wickham claims you have his child. Is this true?"

Elizabeth wished William could lie, but anyone who saw the baby would know she was Georgiana's daughter. Elizabeth had known immediately.

"There is a child," Darcy said.

"I knew it!" Wickham said. Elizabeth imagined him pointing his finger at William when he added, "He is trying to cheat me out of my inheritance by keeping my child as his own."

Elizabeth clenched her hands at her sides. Someone needed to smack some sense into that selfish coward. Given the opportunity, she would be the first to volunteer.

Mr. Hanslock said, "I am aware that Mrs.

Wickham resided with you at Pemberley until her recent death. She did not die of consumption, did she?"

"No." William volunteered no extra information, and Elizabeth applauded him for it. She could not see Mr. Hanslock's expression, but she sensed he was enjoying himself. If he was as Mrs. Reynolds claimed him to be, he would enjoy dragging her husband's name through the mire. But would he see justice done? That was all Elizabeth cared about. She and William would endure his slights if he was reasonable for Anne's sake.

"Am I to understand that you have misled others regarding the cause of her demise?" he asked.

Surely, the magistrate knew the answer. Why would he ask such a thing unless he meant to be cruel?

"My sister died after giving birth. I acted out of respect for her wishes," William replied.

"And the child survived?" the magistrate asked.

"Yes."

Elizabeth heard the smirk on Mr. Hanslock's face as he said, "Even if Mrs. Wickham were to assign you guardianship over her child, she did not have the authority to do so while her husband lives. The laws favor the rights of the father, as I am certain you are very well aware, Mr. Darcy."

Lying and breaking the law. Mr. Hanslock must be gloating. He sounded as though he was.

Clamping her lips shut and crossing her arms over her chest, Elizabeth constrained her rage. Had there been a pistol at hand, she might have shot Wickham and put an end to the obstacle between them and Anne's guardianship.

Wickham and William were opposites. Wickham had done nothing to recover his wife when he heard of her illness while William had married a stranger to keep his promise. Already, Elizabeth was considering drastic measures. How far would she go to help him?

Maybe it was to her advantage there were no dueling pistols in sight. Neither was there a sword hanging over the fire mantel. She had looked.

And how dare Mr. Hanslock speak to her husband of the laws of Chancery when William probably knew more about the laws regarding guardians and their wards than the Lord Chancellor did at this point.

Mr. Hanslock continued, "Then, you know you have no recourse. You will have to hand the child over to the father."

Silence. Elizabeth thought her heart would burst.

"If I refuse?" William asked.

Elizabeth raised her fist in the air. That was her William!

"Then I will arrest you right now and take the child by force."

She dropped her fist.

Evelyn wrapped her arm around Elizabeth's. "Oh, Mrs. Darcy, I am so sorry. Mr. Wickham is not a good man. He will not give Baby Anne the proper care. Oh, this is awful! They will force you to hand her over!"

Elizabeth found herself in the role of comforter to her lady's maid, patting her hand and shushing her while Elizabeth's mind buzzed.

What if William had no choice? What if he had to give Anne to Wickham? Elizabeth could break into Wickham's rooms at the inn to steal Anne away during the night. She had stabbed the hat pin through her bodice in anticipation of his call that morning, securing it against her corset so that it looked like an embellishment. Should Elizabeth need it, she was ready. She only needed an excuse.

Evelyn hiccupped through her tears, lamenting, "What does Mr. Wickham know of caring for an infant? She will cry, and he will not know what to do. How will he feed her? I doubt he even has a nurse. I know little enough about babies, but I am convinced I know more than he does. Oh, this is a disaster!"

Time froze. Had there been a break in the clouds, its hopeful rays would have shown through the windows of the antechamber. Spinning to face Evelyn, Elizabeth grabbed the girl and kissed her cheek. "That is right! It *is* a disaster. You are brilliant, Evelyn!"

Charging out of the room, Elizabeth intercepted the gentlemen before they could take one step inside Pemberley's hall. "Excuse me, please, but might I have a word?" she asked.

Ever the gentleman, William (who did not look at all surprised to see her) introduced Elizabeth to the magistrate.

He was a wiry man with a hawkish nose and sharp eyes, and at a glance, Elizabeth determined she did not like him.

Organizing her arguments while she curtsied, Elizabeth began, "It is an honor to meet you, Mr. Hanslock. I trust that a sagacious gentleman with your experience will agree with me when I express certain concerns regarding the child's immediate removal from Pemberley."

"The child is mine! You cannot keep him from me." Wickham tried to push past William, to no avail.

Elizabeth's jaw tightened, and she fingered the beads of her hat pin, but she kept her calm. Addressing Mr. Hanslock, she said, "There is your first proof, sir. Mr. Wickham does not even know the sex of his child, wrongly assuming he fathered a boy when the infant is a girl. A dear, sweet, delicate girl who requires the services of a wet nurse besides all of the usual accoutrements an infant needs." When the magistrate's features did not soften, she focused once again on the practical. "Did Mr. Wickham bring a nurse with him?"

Mr. Hanslock's lips tightened in annoyance, but he asked Wickham, "Do you have a nurse waiting at the inn?"

"I will employ one as soon as we return."

Elizabeth shook her head. "As I am certain you well know, a wet nurse is not always an easy person to find on short notice as she usually has children of her own to tend to or is already in service to another family. Is Mr. Wickham planning on staying in Lambton, or does he plan on leaving?"

Mr. Hanslock looked to Wickham for an answer.

"I would not dream of staying longer than necessary. I will hire a nurse as soon as we reach London," Wickham huffed.

He played into Elizabeth's hand much better than she could have hoped for. "Your plan is to starve your daughter for days? Are you not aware of how often an infant nurses? I have to wonder what else you do not know, Mr. Wickham." Again, she addressed Mr. Hanslock. "Clearly, this matter was not thought through. Of course, I do not mean to imply you, Mr. Hanslock, but rather Mr. Wickham, who ought to have taken measures toward the comfort of his own daughter if, indeed, he intends to take on the responsibility of her care. I beg of you not to cause the infant any more discomfort than she will have to endure with such an ignorant father." Elizabeth bit her tongue. She really ought not insult Wickham, but he made it so easy.

Mr. Hanslock puffed out his chest, standing taller. "I am under no obligation to you, Mrs. Darcy. My duty, first and foremost, is to restore the child to her proper place — to her father. However…"

Elizabeth held her breath, silently praying for Mr. Hanslock to be reasonable.

He continued, "…it is clear to me that Mr. Wickham is not prepared to take proper care of his child, and I cannot rightly insist that Mr. Darcy hand the infant over until I see for myself that her needs can be met."

Wickham's face burned in open hatred. "I demand to take her with me now."

Elizabeth said, "In one week's time. That will give

you sufficient time to find a nurse and purchase what your daughter will need. Anything less would be impossible."

Directing his hawkish glare at her, Mr. Hanslock said, "I will allow until the morrow for Mr. Wickham to make preparations. Do not see this as a victory, Mrs. Darcy. Both you and Mr. Darcy must be made to see that you are not above the law. You must pay for your crimes. We will return on the morrow, and you will hand the child over to Mr. Wickham without any trouble or further arguments."

One day.

They had one day.

CHAPTER 30

"We could sail to America. Or Australia. Whichever has a ship leaving first," Elizabeth suggested, twirling a loose strand of hair between her fingers as she chewed on her bottom lip. Her gaze traveled through the room, and she added under her breath, "It will be a pity to leave behind such a wonderful library."

Darcy wiped the jar of preserves clean with the last piece of shortbread. Handing it to her, he said, "I am glad we wed before you saw my library, or I would forever suspect you married me for my collection of books."

"A lady must have priorities." She smiled, nibbled on the shortbread, then handed it back to him. "Please have the rest. I cannot eat another bite."

"Good because the tray is empty."

Elizabeth's eyes widened. "How long have we been in here?"

Darcy looked at the mantel clock. "It is nearly midnight."

She sighed. "And we are no closer to saving Anne than we were hours ago. What are we going to do, William?"

He looked at the tower of bills he had collected over the past year. Pointing at it, he said, "That is our best option. I will show Mr. Hanslock Wickham's unpaid bills. We can argue that without my occasional interference (which I only did while my sister was alive), he will soon end up in debtor's prison."

"Mr. Hanslock will not care. Children are raised within the prison walls all the time. He will not pity Anne."

Darcy agreed, but he had one more argument. "I also possess quite a collection of Wickham's unpaid debts. I mean to offer to settle them in exchange for his signature assigning guardianship to me."

"He will never agree to it. Not when he has a foothold on Pemberley."

"No, but we will try. There is nothing else. It is a pity that even inept fathers have more rights than we do, but it is the law."

Elizabeth huffed. "Chancery laws offend my

sense of justice. I hear Australia has rather large snakes. I do not know if I could ever feel comfortable in a country with serpents that can eat crocodiles."

Darcy adored his wife's willingness to explore more drastic solutions, but it would not do. "They would stop us before we reached the coast. Even if we did make it aboard ship, would you spend the rest of our lives on the run? You would never see your family again."

Elizabeth shrugged, then her brow furrowed. "I would miss Jane."

"And your father?" Darcy asked.

She scrunched her nose. "I will forgive him … eventually. It is not in my nature to be angry for longer than necessary."

"I am grateful for that," Darcy teased.

"Come," she said, grabbing a lit candle and standing, "let us check on Anne again."

"We will wake Mrs. Bamber."

Elizabeth's eyes teared. "She will not mind, I think. This could be Anne's last night with us."

Not if Darcy could help it. He only prayed that Wickham's greed exceeded his sense of entitlement, or he would never sign away what he considered to be his rightful inheritance.

Darcy reached for Elizabeth's hand, holding it

close to him as they went up the flight of steps and down the hall to Anne's nursery.

Opening the door slowly, so as not to startle Mrs. Bamber or wake Anne, Darcy tip-toed over the carpet after Elizabeth. Should he tell her how much he admired her tonight? How deeply he loved her? Darcy had seen Elizabeth at her worst — betrayed, hurt, and grieving. The challenges they had faced had revealed her character, and Darcy thought her exquisite. Matchless. He could travel the world and live a thousand years, and he would not find another like Elizabeth. He loved her. He was going to tell her.

Touching her elbow, the words he burned to tell her on the tip of his tongue, he waited for her to turn to him.

She spun. "She is gone!" Elizabeth gasped.

Darcy's mouth went dry.

"William, she is gone!" she repeated, looking about frantically.

Anne. Where was Anne? He threw her blanket to the side. She was not there. He looked around the room for any sign of Anne, but she was nowhere in sight. The window was ajar…. He opened it, leaning out and squinting his eyes in the dark. Nothing.

"Mrs. Bamber is gone," Elizabeth said, her hand over her mouth and her chest heaving.

It was Darcy's worst nightmare come to life. His

failure toward Georgiana was nothing compared to this. Anne had been kidnapped one floor above him in his own home.

Think. He needed to think. "Mrs. Bamber would never take Anne away."

"Not even to keep her from Wickham?"

Wickham. The fiend who had stolen Georgiana out from under Darcy's nose as smoothly as a fox sneaking into a chicken coop. Had he been too impatient to wait until the morrow?

Darcy straightened. "First, we must search the house. Anne is a secret no more."

Elizabeth squeezed his hand. "I will wake the servants."

An hour later, every nook and crevice of Pemberley had been searched. Anne was gone.

Darcy gritted his teeth. He knew where to find her. "Ready a horse. I am going to the inn," he told Grayson.

"For me, too," Elizabeth said, adding, "I am not letting you go alone."

"Do you ride?" Darcy asked. He would not travel slowly.

"I will keep up. We cannot allow that horrible man to slip away from us with Anne. We might never see her again."

Darcy's thoughts exactly.

Icy rain stung his face, but he pushed onward, galloping as fast as his horse could carry him over the slippery road to Lambton. To the inn. To Wickham.

True to her word, Elizabeth kept up.

All of the inn's upstairs windows were dark, but Wickham would not be sleeping. If he was there. He might already be in a coach carrying him away from Derbyshire.

Flinging his horse's reins around a post, Darcy charged inside. Wickham sat at a table with four other men, empty glasses, piled banknotes, and scattered coins surrounding them. He jolted to attention so quickly, he upset his chair when Darcy burst into the taproom.

"Give her back!" Darcy demanded.

"Give who back?" Wickham asked, righting his chair and stuffing the banknotes in front of him in his pocket.

Darcy charged toward Wickham, grabbing him by the collar. The ne'er-do-well wreaked of spirits. "Anne! Where is she?"

Wickham's eyes widened. Even drunk, he was an amazing actor. He always had been. "I do not know what you are talking about, but if you have lost my child, then it is I who ought to be making demands and accusations. Call the magistrate to arrest this man!" he demanded of nobody in particular.

Not one man moved. They huddled together on the opposite side of the table.

Darcy was not intimidated. "You kidnapped her. You could not find a nurse, and you took matters into your own hands before Mr. Hanslock could stop you. Where are you hiding her?" He raised his fist.

Wickham shrank in Darcy's hand, his eyes wide and wild. "I swear on my life I do not have her. You have to believe me, Darcy."

"Why should I ever believe you?" Darcy seethed.

"Look in my room. Search all of my possessions. Ask these men if I have been here all night."

Darcy looked at the men grouped around the table. They all shook their heads enthusiastically.

A voice from the top of the stairs exclaimed, "Good God, Darcy, what has happened? You look like the devil."

Mr. Gardiner stood at the top of the landing in his night cap and robe. Mrs. Gardiner stood behind him, one hand over her mouth and the other gripping her husband's arm.

Darcy lowered his fist. He did, however, push Wickham away, sending him sprawling over the floor.

While Darcy was disinclined to trust Wickham's word, he was not completely without reason. Anne would have cried by now. Someone would have noticed her if she were in the building. Had Wickham meant to kidnap her, Darcy would not have found him at leisure, playing cards at the inn.

Elizabeth asked her uncle, "Have you noticed anything untoward tonight? Anne is gone. Kidnapped."

Mr. Gardiner shook his head. "I only retired an hour ago, and I can assure you that until the time I entered my room, Mr. Wickham was in the taproom with these men."

Mrs. Gardiner stepped out from behind him. "Who is Anne?"

Darcy answered, "She is my niece. Georgiana's child. I promised my sister I would take care of her; that I would protect her child from this man."

"How can we help you?" asked Mr. Gardiner, taking off his cap and smoothing his hair.

Freed from Darcy's hold, Wickham staggered to his feet. Pulling a flask from his waistcoat pocket, he tossed back a heavy dose of its contents. In a more courageous tone, he said, "I see what is happening. You are hiding her from me so you do not have to hand her over on the morrow. You took everything from me, and now I will take everything from you. Pemberley is as good as mine."

Darcy ignored him. He had more urgent matters on his mind than Wickham's threats. What was Pemberley if his family was not complete?

Elizabeth, however, was not done with the ingrate. "Have you no pride? No honor? Your daughter is lost, kidnapped, and you do nothing to find her? You would rather breathe threats? Did you even bother to hire a nurse for your daughter?" she hissed.

Wickham's lack of a reply made Darcy sick.

They searched Wickham's room, and when the groom confirmed that no horse or carriage had passed him that evening bearing Wickham either to or from Pemberley, Darcy and Elizabeth had no alternative but to return to Pemberley.

As impossible as it was for anyone other than Wickham to have taken Anne, that was precisely what had happened.

Where was Anne?

CHAPTER 31

*E*lizabeth shivered in her damp redingote. The gown she had been wearing since the day before clung to her legs, tripping her whenever she dismounted her horse to walk. She clenched her teeth together lest William saw them chatter. He would send her back to Pemberley to warm herself, and Elizabeth would not have it. Not when he had to be every bit as cold and miserable as she was. Until they found Anne, there was no excuse to give up their search.

If Anne was in the vicinity of Pemberley, they would find her. Riders had been sent to make inquiries farther down the roads. Neighbors Elizabeth had yet to meet offered their assistance. Loudest among them was Mrs. Bamber and her tribe of nine children. On leaving the inn, Elizabeth and William had ridden in the direction of Mrs. Bamber's house. They had met her on the path, walking like a general charging into battle with her troops trailing behind her. She had heard the news.

"I will find her," she repeated with such a fierce look and harsh tone, Elizabeth doubted Mrs. Bamber spoke of the baby.

"What do you know?" William had asked.

"I know nothing, and that is the truth of it. But Lord help her if I find her." She continued walking, the unstoppable determination on her face firmly in place.

Several times, Elizabeth tried to extract more information, but Mrs. Bamber marched onward like a horse wearing blinkers.

William, knowing his time was better spent elsewhere, rode from cluster to cluster of searchers.

That had been hours ago, and Elizabeth had lost Mrs. Bamber in the crowd of helpers. The sun rose, and while it did not warm their backs, it illuminated their path. It did not, however, light their way to Anne.

Elizabeth saw William near a copse of trees, and she rode to him. Her fingers were so cold, it was painful to move them over the reins. She prayed Anne was warm.

"Any news?" she asked, the slump in William's shoulders dashing her hope before he said a word.

He ran his hand over his face. "No. Let us ride to the house. Perhaps they have had better success."

What if they did not find Anne? What if they did find her only to have Wickham take her away that same day? Elizabeth acknowledged the helplessness of their situation, but she refused to bow before it. The blow to William would be irreparable, and she loved him too much to allow it.

Shouts of "Anne!" echoed over the fields. They would find her. They *had* to find her. The kindness of their servants and neighbors, their tireless efforts to help them find a babe they did not know existed until that day, gave Elizabeth heart. She said, "All these people have been so generous helping us. We should offer them something to eat."

"I have already asked Mrs. Reynolds to open the kitchens."

Elizabeth was not surprised William had already seen to the needs of others. He always did.

They rode silently, too tired and discouraged to pretend cheer. Elizabeth's humor failed her. If this was what life was like without Anne, Elizabeth would fight tooth and nail to keep Wickham from taking her away ... if they found her.

Maybe better news awaited them at the house. She clung to the possibility.

An elegant carriage sat in the drive. Elizabeth did not recognize it, but given William's open mouth, he clearly did.

"What? Who is it?" she asked.

He shook his head. "I told her she could come, but I never thought she would do it. She must like you as much as she loved my mother."

Madame Givenchy appeared at the top of the steps. Two footmen unloaded a large trunk from her carriage and carried it inside.

Handing off their horses, William and Elizabeth climbed the steps to meet her.

Madame clucked her tongue. "I leave scandalous London for the fresh country air, and I see Pemberley is in an upheaval."

"I am afraid you have come at a difficult time, but you are always welcome at Pemberley," William said, taking her proffered hand and leading her inside.

"Tut, tut. There is always time to look one's best." The proprietress turned to Elizabeth, looking her up and down with a firm scowl. "This is not your best. You need a bath. Where is your maid?"

Elizabeth opened her mouth to speak, but she could give no answer. Where was Evelyn? Come to think of it, she had not seen Evelyn all morning.

When *had* she last seen her? "I do not know. I do not recall seeing her."

Where was Evelyn?

Elizabeth's eyes met William's.

He said, "She heard Mrs. Bamber's threats to steal Anne away. Do you think she might have done it?"

Exactly what Elizabeth had been thinking. Mrs. Bamber's reaction made much more sense now. She had not been talking about Anne, but about Evelyn. Elizabeth's pulse raced. "She is loyal enough to the family to attempt it."

Madame Givenchy inclined her head to something on the other side of the open doors. "Is that the cause of all this commotion?"

A baby cried.

William and Elizabeth ran outside and down the steps.

Mrs. Bamber, red-faced and notably agitated, pulled a weeping Evelyn by the arm. The girl's frantic apologies were audible over the wails of the unhappy baby she held. "I am so sorry! I only thought to help, but she will not stop crying, and I do not know how to soothe her."

"She is probably hungry and frightened," Elizabeth exclaimed, relief tempering her anger. "Really, Evelyn, what were you thinking?"

William took Anne, humming as he rocked her in

his arms. Anne reached her little fingers up to brush against his unshaved chin. He would not give her up. If Wickham wanted to take Anne from Pemberley, he would have to pry her out of William's arms first ... if he could get past Elizabeth.

First things first. Elizabeth embraced William and Anne, enveloping the baby with all the love Elizabeth longed to give her own children. Anne's fuzzy, fine hair tickled her nose from under her cap, but Elizabeth would not dream of moving when she felt the baby's chubby hand caressing her cheek. It was easy to forget they could not remain in each other's arms forever, but she had to deal with Evelyn.

The maid continued apologizing, wiping her face and sniffing her swollen, red nose.

Evelyn continued, "I heard Mr. Wickham's threats, and if you ask me, he is greedy enough to be capable of sneaking into Pemberley to take the child. I could not bear to think of you losing her when it is plain to everyone how much you both love her — especially Mr. Darcy. He is a better father than Mr. Wickham could ever be. He loves Baby Anne as much as I have ever seen any father dote on his own child. Mrs. Bamber gave me the idea."

"Do not mention my name, you foolish girl," Mrs. Bamber said, taking Anne and pushing Evelyn forward. To William and Elizabeth, she said, "I apologize for not voicing my suspicion sooner, but I knew this girl was silly enough to risk her own life for your benefit without any regard for the consequences. She has no sense at all and does not know the first thing about babies. I found her crouched behind a barrel in the wine cellar, of all places. Now, if you will excuse me, I must see to Anne's needs. The poor dear is starving. I will answer your questions once she is fed and sleeping."

Evelyn spilled her confession without enticement. "It is true. I am a fool. I lied to Mrs. Bamber. She asked me to stay with Anne while she saw to nature's call. That was when it occurred to me. I thought that if I just kept Little Anne away until Mr. Wickham left, then she could stay." She sniffed and snorted until William handed her his handkerchief.

"How did you convince Mrs. Bamber to leave?" he asked.

Evelyn hiccupped. "I ran into Mrs. Darcy's bedchamber and grabbed the biggest, shiniest necklace I could find. Babies like shiny things. That, I know. Then, I left Anne in a pile of blankets in the middle of the bed with the necklace to entertain her while I ran back to the nursery."

Elizabeth gasped. "You left Anne unattended? She could have toppled off the bed! Or rolled too close to the fire."

"I thought of that later, and I have decided I am not fit to have children."

William snapped, his patience clearly reaching its limit. "How on earth did you get Mrs. Bamber to leave Anne with you?"

"I did not have to. When she came back, I told her that Mrs. Darcy had suggested that Mrs. Bamber go home for the night. That since it was their last night with Anne, she wanted Anne with her in her room. Right then, Anne made a happy sort of noise from the direction of Mrs. Darcy's bedchamber. It was perfect, really, if you ask me," she whimpered.

Evelyn's heart was clearly bigger than her sense, and Elizabeth could not find it in her to punish the girl for it.

Holding her cold hands over her burning cheeks, Elizabeth said, "Oh, Evelyn. What am I supposed to do with you?"

The girl looked down at her hands. "Mrs. Bamber said she would take a switch to me if I showed my face in her nursery ever again. I will pack my things and leave. I am not fit to serve here."

"You will do no such thing."

William must have agreed. He said, "We will discuss the matter once our nerves have calmed."

Elizabeth sighed in relief. The footman who had

accompanied her to Hatchards was still in his employ. Evelyn's position was safe.

He continued, "Now, we ought to begin spreading the word to all who have helped us and invite them for a repast." To Elizabeth, William said, "We have a call to prepare for."

Elizabeth shivered. She wished both to delay the call so it would never come and to rush through it so it would already be done.

Madame Givenchy moved between Elizabeth and Evelyn. Looping her arms between theirs, she said, "It is good I am here. I come to Pemberley, and *poof!* The baby is found! Everyone is happy. Now, please come with me so you can explain what has happened and allow me prepare you for this call. It is a bad one, *oui?*"

"The worst. Too much depends on our success," Elizabeth replied.

Madame smiled. "Ah, then you must dress like the victor you need to be. You will present yourself in your finest. And I have just the thing."

CHAPTER 32

"*W*ickham will not arrive any sooner for all your pacing, Darcy." Mr. Gardiner sat beside his wife in the drawing room where they waited.

Darcy tried to sit, but he popped out of his seat again when Madame Givenchy appeared in the doorway.

"*Mes amis*, my friends, allow me to present my newest creation," she said, stepping aside for Elizabeth.

Darcy's breath slowed — if, indeed, he remembered to breathe at all. He could not look away, nor did he blink lest he miss a moment.

"She is stunning, *oui?*"

Elizabeth was a vision adorned with glimmering forest green silk. Her cheeks blushed the color of rose petals, and her fine eyes brightened when she met his gaze. Darcy nodded, unable to speak.

Grayson cleared his throat. "Mr. Hanslock is here with Mr. Wickham."

Darcy resented the intrusion when he would much rather appreciate his wife. Offering Elizabeth his arm, he said, "You are beautiful."

She smiled at him. "I could take down Napoleon in this gown. Wickham has nothing against us."

Their victory would not be easily won, but defeat was unacceptable. Darcy's family was whole. He was whole. To lose Anne today would be to lose everything he had sacrificed so much for all over again.

Taking his position beside the fireplace with Elizabeth seated beside him, Darcy said, "Show them in."

Wickham sauntered in. "Did you find my daughter?" he asked before he had taken his seat.

"No thanks to you," Elizabeth snapped.

"So, she is returned. I am not surprised you came to your senses and found her in time for our meeting. How convenient," he retorted.

"Enough," Mr. Hanslock commanded. "Where is the child?"

Darcy rested his hand on Elizabeth's shoulder. She squeezed it in support.

Mr. and Mrs. Gardiner, too, held on to each other on the couch where they sat.

"Anne is with her nurse," he replied.

"Bring her down. Mr. Wickham has secured everything she requires, and if you will hand over the child, our business here can come to an end." Mr. Hanslock spoke as dryly as one would negotiating a transaction at a bank.

Darcy nodded to Grayson, who hovered by the door.

While they waited for Mrs. Bamber to join them with Anne, Darcy pulled out the receipts he had been accumulating over the year Georgiana was married to Wickham. It was a sizable collection.

"There is one matter I must draw to your attention." He handed the stack of papers to Mr. Hanslock, who leafed through them.

"I thought I was clear. I do not wish to hear any more arguments. The child belongs to Mr. Wickham."

"What I present are facts, and they have a direct influence on Anne. As such, they are worthy of your attention. Those are the bills I have paid during the time Mr. Wickham was married to my sister."

Mr. Hanslock tossed the papers on the table. "So Mr. Wickham has a habit of accumulating debts and trusting others to cover them for him. I do not see how that makes him any different from most other gentlemen."

"You are willing to allow him to raise his daughter in debtor's prison?" asked Elizabeth.

"Why should his daughter be spared when so many other children are raised within the prison's walls?"

Mr. Hanslock would not be moved.

Wickham looked smug. He was not concerned in the least. He had nothing to lose and everything to gain while Anne's future hung in the balance. Was there nothing Darcy could use to level the field?

Darcy tried again. Producing another mound of bills and handing them to Wickham, he said, "These are not paid. Look through them. Ensure they are all yours." He wanted Wickham to see the reality of his debts — to make a man who lived for the moment fear the future.

Wickham chuckled. "All this tells me is that I have lived well. What is wrong with that?"

"It is wrong when it threatens those for whom you are responsible."

He shrugged. "The shops will be eager to lend to me when they find out I will inherit the Darcy fortune."

"Your daughter. Anne. Not you," Elizabeth retorted.

Another shrug. "Is there any difference?"

Darcy knew what the answer would be before he asked, but he would attempt the unlikely. "I will offer to cover your debts — all of them. You can leave here knowing no creditors will bother you or send their thugs out to hunt you down. I will even give you an additional five hundred pounds for you to live on as long as you are able."

Wickham leaned forward, his eyes gleaming. "To what do I credit this sudden generosity? What do you get for this exchange?"

"You sign Anne's guardianship over to me."

Leaning back and crossing a booted foot over his knee, Wickham laughed. "That is rich! As if I would tempted to give up this?" He waved his arm about him.

Elizabeth stood, and Darcy grabbed her hand lest she attack Wickham. "Do you not see the advantage to you? Are you so confident you will inherit? I could be with child at this moment."

That got Wickham's attention. "Are you?" he asked.

The room fell silent.

Mrs. Gardiner clutched her fichu.

Darcy clenched his jaw. That had been the one argument he had not been willing to address — for Elizabeth's sake and for his own. Wickham had already dealt treacherously with his family. Who was to say he would not do it again? They would never be free of Wickham. They would forever have to look over their shoulders.

Lifting her chin, Elizabeth said, "It is too soon to know, but all it would take is one child, and your chances of getting anything are gone. What will you do with Anne then?"

The chill in Wickham's voice sent needles prickling down Darcy's spine. "The chances of you producing an heir are about as high as Darcy's meeting a premature death, I would say. Besides, the women in this household do not often survive childbirth."

Darcy's voice shook as he addressed Mr. Hanslock. "You would trust a man with the life of a small child when he clearly threatens me and my wife?"

Wickham scoffed. "It is a fact. Can you deny the cause of your mother and sister's deaths? Will you claim to be immortal when many of our Cambridge chums are dead from sickness or some accident?"

Mr. Hanslock frowned. "What Mr. Wickham says is true."

Had the man no feeling at all?

He continued, "My position as magistrate demands I uphold and enforce the law. I will see your daughter restored to you, Mr. Wickham, as she is yours to maintain. No man is above the law, and Mr. Darcy will suffer the consequences of his offense. However, I will warn you. Stay out of Derbyshire. If any accident should befall the Darcys, you would be the first person I would suspect."

While Darcy appreciated Mr. Hanslock's display of sense, it did not change anything. They were going to lose Anne. Darcy tried to keep his composure, but he nearly broke down when Mrs. Bamber appeared with his niece just then.

"Ah, my beautiful daughter. The image of her mother, I think," said Wickham. He did not rise from his chair or move to hold his offspring. While Darcy was glad of it, it was another proof in the long list of reasons why Wickham ought not to be entrusted with her.

Elizabeth's arm slipped around William's waist. He wrapped his arm around her shoulders, pressing her to his side, grateful for her strength when his world once again threatened to crumble.

Wickham leaned forward, tapping his fingers together. "You have made your arguments, and they have been rebutted. Now, allow me to make a counteroffer. I will sign Anne over to you, witnessed by the magistrate himself so that it is beyond contestation."

Darcy listened with baited breath and a hammering heart.

"I see I have your attention, as well I should when I can give you everything you want. You wish to honor your promise to Georgiana and raise her child? I will allow it. On one condition."

He paused.

If Darcy spoke, he would betray his eagerness. Elizabeth, too, tightened her grip around Darcy's waist, but she did not say anything. He nodded for Wickham to continue.

Rubbing his hands together, Wickham said, "I will give you Anne's guardianship if you swear to me before this room of witnesses that you will separate from your wife. You must never have children. It is that simple really: Anne or your wife. You must choose."

Darcy had gone to great lengths to prove himself unlike Wickham, and now the fiend would have him betray his wife? To act as Mr. Bennet had toward the daughter he had claimed to love? No. A million times, no.

Filled with renewed ire, Darcy growled, "How dare you demand that I choose between a niece I adore and a wife I love with all my heart. I will never stop fighting to keep Anne, but I will not break the vows I gave to Elizabeth. I love her."

CHAPTER 33

*E*lizabeth's heart skipped, and she bit her cheeks to keep from smiling. Her glee was great, but she could not display her happiness with Wickham in the room.

William loved her! He would not trade her for his heart's desire. *She* was his heart's desire!

She looked up at William, waiting until he met her gaze before saying, "And I love you."

Like a menacing cloud intent on raining on Elizabeth's parade, Wickham stood to his feet and pointed at William. "You fool! I will take everything from you just as you have denied me of that which ought to be mine."

Elizabeth saw a sparkle. She blinked to ensure it was real. Still there. She had not noticed it before, but it was plain to see the pillow-shaped diamond pierced in the center of his cravat now. It was an unusual cut. She knew where she had seen it before.

How had it come to be in Wickham's possession?

Her body fluttered with nervous excitement; it was difficult to think clearly. Could it be that simple?

Elizabeth glanced at her aunt. She wished she could ask her about the article she had read the day before in the paper. Had the stolen jewels belonged to the wealthy widow with whom Wickham had been riding in the carriage?

Was Wickham a jewel thief? All of their problems would be settled if she could prove he was. Mr. Hanslock took his duties too seriously to overlook such a crime. And while he would permit Anne to be raised in a debtor's prison, Newgate was another matter entirely.

Elizabeth's mind hummed. Where was the proof?

First, there was Wickham's history of entitlement. That was a good one; it established motive.

Second, he had a history of theft. Aunt Gardiner had told them that, and she was present to confirm it. Good.

Now, that left the wealthy widow. A woman such as she would not shy away from the attention the papers would give her if her jewels were stolen. In fact, Elizabeth imagined that a woman such as she would enjoy the attention. All they had to do was ask her directly…. What a pity London was not closer to Pemberley.

What of Wickham's complete disregard for William's generous offer? He had not been tempted at all. Could that be because he already had a supply of money by selling the widow's cut up diamond necklace?

It was not enough evidence to convince a jury, but it was enough to convince Elizabeth.

Wickham continued, "Is it not enough that you flaunt your wealth and privilege in my face? I am not so destitute as you believe me to be. Your threats mean nothing to me."

As if to reaffirm Elizabeth's suspicions, he spun the diamond between his fingers.

It was time to voice her suspicion.

"You are not destitute you say? And yet, my husband has presented you with a stack of bills representing a small fortune."

Wickham's face turned red and he sat. "I will manage as I always do."

"Yes, I have heard how you manage. Stealing is hardly the solution."

Mr. Hanslock shot her a stern look. "That is a serious accusation, Mrs. Darcy."

"Lies. I could equally accuse you of stealing my daughter," snapped Wickham.

Elizabeth would finish what she had started. She continued, "I have it on excellent authority that over the years you have stolen several items from the shop at Lambton."

Aunt nodded her support.

Wickham snarled, "That was years ago. You can hardly hold me accountable for something that was settled so long ago."

"So, you admit it. Thank you, Mr. Wickham," Elizabeth said, growing in confidence when she saw how intently Mr. Hanslock listened. "Stealing little trifles is not enough anymore, though, is it? Your debts are so grand, you woo your way into the confidence of wealthy widows, then take their jewels."

"Absurd!" Wickham cried.

"Is it? I saw that same diamond on a lady's necklace in London. You stole it from her, and you have been using the money from the gemstones to pay off your debts. Can you deny it?" Elizabeth watched the magistrate and Wickham.

The thief stood. "This is absurd! Hand over my child. I wish to leave."

"Sit down, Mr. Wickham," Mr. Hanslock ordered. "I am well enough aware of your habits to doubt your sudden change of fortune. How did you come to possess the diamond in your cravat?"

Wickham sat down stiffly. "It was given to me by a lady as a gift. It is mine."

"What is the lady's name?" Elizabeth asked, her gaze now bouncing between Wickham and her aunt, who would surely react when she heard him pronounce the name of the lady about whom she had read in the paper.

"That is no concern of yours. The lady gave them to me. She can have no interest in what I choose to do with them now that they are mine."

Madame Givenchy stepped forward. "Oh, but you are wrong, Mr. Wickham. Her ladyship is very much interested."

Elizabeth felt ten feet tall. This was it! Wickham would be charged with the theft of the wealthy widow's jewels. All they had to do was charge him with the crime, and the courts would take care of the rest. He would have to sign Anne over or else give her to Chancery. Her stomach clenched. Oh, no, that would not do. He would sooner let Chancery find a place for Anne than leave her with them. He would do it out of pure spite.

The reeling of her mind came to an abrupt halt when Madame Givenchy said, "Her ladyship's name is Lady Priscilla. Her husband died one year ago."

"We will write to her immediately—" Elizabeth began.

Madame interrupted. "I am afraid it would do no good. You see, Lady Priscilla recently had some gowns made by me, and I am apprised of her ... shall we call them ... paramours? I can confirm that Lady Priscilla did, in fact, give her diamonds to this man."

Elizabeth steadied herself against William's arm. Her heart dropped, but she would hold herself upright.

It could not be.

Madame smiled coyly. "Ah, but there are other secrets worth more than diamond necklaces, *oui?*"

Wickham's face blanched, and he wiped his forehead. He was worried.

"Her ladyship already has several gowns ready for her return to society next week," Madame explained. "I know because I made them. They are divinely scandalous. She will be all the rage."

Where was Madame going with this?

"There is no reason to bring Lady Priscilla into this." Wickham crossed his feet, attempting to look unaffected.

Oh, but he was very affected. Madame was on to something, and Elizabeth only waited to know what it was so she could gain them some advantage over him. Anything they could use to bargain for Anne.

Madame tapped her fingers against her chin, reveling in the attention. "I wonder how Lady

Priscilla will like having to share the attention of her betrothed with the baby of his first wife."

"Betrothed?" William gasped.

Madame gasped, daintily covering her lips with her fingers. "Did I say that? It was supposed to be a secret."

How about that? Secrets had created this mess, and it looked like Wickham's secret might help them secure Anne.

CHAPTER 34

*D*arcy knew Wickham had married Georgiana for her dowry, but the news of his engagement to another wealthy benefactress felt like a slap in the face of his sister's memory. Georgie had only been gone three months.

He knew Madame Givenchy had given them a valuable piece of information, but his thoughts were too conflicted to focus on how best to exploit it for Anne's benefit.

Not so with Elizabeth. She said, "I wonder what Lady Priscilla will think of Mr. Wickham when she discovers he is using her to pay his debts? That she will not only have to pay for his keep, but for that of his child?"

Mrs. Gardiner opined, "One might draw the conclusion that Mr. Wickham's affection was not so strong as his need for money. If her ladyship married for security the first time, surely, she wishes to marry for love the second."

"She will not be affected. You think you have something on me, but you do not, so you had best guard your silence," Wickham hissed.

Darcy was ready to rise in Mrs. Gardiner's defense, but the lady smiled at him softly through her pinched lips. What did she know?

Elizabeth tilted her head. "Really? She will not be affected? I do not hold any delusions that you intend to take your daughter into your home, Mr. Wickham, but I have to wonder if you have truly considered the cost of raising a child. Even if you hand her off to another family, you will be responsible for her clothing, food, instruction…," she counted on her fingers. "Too many things to mention, but you will have to foot the bill for every single one of them until the day Anne marries."

Darcy understood her. If she turned the advantage Wickham thought he had into a responsibility, he might not want it anymore. Judging from Mr. Hanslock's nod, Elizabeth's assumptions were correct. More than that, Wickham had to be forced to see he could not have both.

"Are you willing to risk the security and comfort you have now for the uncertain prospect of inheriting years — decades — from now? You gamble enough to know the odds are not in your favor," Darcy added.

It was plain Wickham thought he could marry his widow, biding his time easily until Pemberley was his. Well, there were many more obstacles in his way than that, and Darcy took pleasure in pointing them out. "You would need to ensure you have enough capital to raise Anne. Children, especially girls, are costly. You could not choose just any family to raise her, if that was your intention. She will have to be brought up as a gentleman's daughter, or your negligence would reflect poorly on you were she ever to inherit. Aside from the constant employ of a nurse, Anne will need a governess, several tutors, and, later when she enters society, a companion."

Elizabeth took his lead and expanded upon it. "Do not forget all the fineries and fripperies a young lady requires. Even a simple wardrobe is costly, and rightly so" — she added with a smile at Madame Givenchy — "as you will find out for yourself soon enough. You will have to ensure Anne is dressed in style. I imagine Lady Priscilla will have opinions about Anne's dowry. If you spread the word that you stand to inherit Pemberley, you will have to put up a pretty sum. Let us hope her ladyship is understanding and generous, or it will fall squarely on your shoulders to maintain your daughter."

Wickham did not squirm in his chair, but he was abnormally still. The thought of spending money on anyone but himself must have been most distasteful.

Watching him, Darcy said, "Anne is not a secret any longer, nor should she remain one. Does Lady Priscilla like children?"

Madame Givenchy answered when Wickham did not. "She despises them."

"How inconvenient for you, Mr. Wickham. I will write to her ladyship today," Elizabeth said, starting as if she meant to perform the task right then.

Wickham dabbed his face when she was partway across the floor.

If they were going to strike, now was the time. Darcy was confident his offer would be tempting, for what did Wickham crave more than instant gratification?

"It is your choice, Wickham. Which will serve you better? The waning possibility of inheriting Pemberley when you are too old to enjoy it or spend your fortune? If you insist on this course, we will inform Lady Priscilla of everything we have discussed here … as well as the other discretions of which we are aware. She will not want you after she learns what we have to tell her. Your life of leisure will be over the moment you set foot outside this house. You can count on it." Darcy paused, letting Wickham sweat. Then, slowly, he added, "I will, however, give you a choice. Sign Anne's guardianship over to me, and we will keep our silence. Anne would no longer be your concern. We will disappear from your life, and you can carry on without the responsibilities which would burden you."

Grayson slipped a piece of paper, a quill pen, and an ink pot onto the table beside Wickham. He had been paying attention.

Mr. Gardiner and his wife leaned forward, watching, waiting.

Madame Givenchy fanned her face, her eyes fixed unblinkingly on Wickham.

Darcy was afraid to breathe lest his and Elizabeth's arguments fall like a house of cards. But he trusted Wickham's greedy nature. He would not want to wait when he could have immediate satisfaction. Darcy was hopeful. Everyone was hopeful. Hopeful and waiting.

Elizabeth's patience ran out. Continuing to the door, she said, "If nothing is to be done here, then I shall start my letter. I have a great deal to write."

Wickham flinched. "You will not tell her ladyship?"

Elizabeth replied, "If you give us Anne's

guardianship, I will not say anything. So far as I am concerned, once you sign that paper, you are no longer her father." She looked at Mr. Hanslock, who offered his view.

"Once you sign over guardianship, you have no claim on your child. It is not a decision to be made hastily."

Darcy bit his lips together when he saw Elizabeth struggle to hide her scowl.

Mr. Gardiner cleared his throat. "Wise advice, but the detriment of many negotiations. One must seize opportunity when it presents itself lest circumstances change — unless you are confident in the constancy of her ladyship's affection. Lady Priscilla has been alone in London for several days now, and she might easily succumb to *ennui*. Worse yet, she may doubt the strength of your affection when you fail to attend to her so soon after she has accepted your offer of marriage. Tarry if you must but know that it is at your own peril."

As uttered by a true businessman. Darcy's respect for Mr. Gardiner now equaled his estimation of Mrs. Gardiner. He was proud to call them family.

Darcy leaned forward, trying not to jump out of his skin when Wickham picked up the quill, dipped it in ink, and signed his name at the bottom of the page.

Before the ink fully dried, Darcy pulled the paper from the table, holding it so as not to smudge the writing. He would not give Wickham the opportunity to change his mind. When it was dry, Darcy folded the precious document and put it into his pocket.

Standing up, Wickham said, "I must leave if I am to depart on the next coach to London."

He bowed, and with Mr. Hanslock, he breezed out of Pemberley.

When the entrance door closed behind the gentlemen, there was great rejoicing in the drawing room.

Elizabeth took Anne from Mrs. Bamber, twirling and dancing around and introducing the babe to her new relatives.

Grayson poured champagne, and Darcy ordered punch for the entire household. It was a day to celebrate.

Once the initial burst of excitement had settled, and they were reliving the scene in conversation again, Elizabeth admitted, "I am not completely satisfied. Wickham's punishment ought to be more severe. I am overjoyed he gave us Anne, but he will leave here to marry his wealthy widow and live a life of leisure and luxury."

To be fair, Darcy's sense of justice was not

entirely satisfied either. But they had Anne. He would have to be content with that.

Madame Givenchy clucked her tongue. "It is not over yet for Mr. Wickham, *mes amis*. He is not the only secret Lady Priscilla keeps."

She had everyone's attention.

Mrs. Gardiner said, "If she is the same lady I have been reading about in the papers, Wickham is in for a horrible surprise when he reaches London. I almost wish we were there to see it," she said.

Madame grinned. "It is she."

"What? What have you read?" Elizabeth asked.

"Lady Priscilla reported her diamonds stolen. It was in the paper this morning."

"Why did you not say so earlier?"

Mrs. Gardiner smiled. "My dear, I wonder why you ask when you heard Mr. Wickham forbid me from speaking with your own ears. What else was I to do but hold my tongue?"

Elizabeth laughed. "I daresay he will find out soon enough."

Madame chuckled. "A clever scheme. Lady Priscilla will use Mr. Wickham to ensure she gets the attention she requires. She does not love him as he believes. She will keep him busy in the courts, and he will keep her name in the papers. She will make him wish he had never been born."

Darcy was satisfied. "She will use him for her pleasure as he has used others for his advantage. I find his upcoming punishment rather appropriate."

IT WAS A BUSY AFTERNOON, and Darcy wanted Anne to have a full share in it. When the weather cleared, they went for a stroll with their party around the gardens, introducing her to everyone they encountered. Anne was the princess of Pemberley. Elizabeth was his queen.

Darcy felt very much like the victorious king with his princess cradled in one arm and his other hand holding his queen. He did not want to leave either of his precious ladies, and so they walked together with the Gardiners around the grounds and through the house. Anne's favorite was the portrait hall where she pounded her fist excitedly against Darcy's shoulder as she smiled at the painting of her mother.

"I wish Anne could know her," Darcy said.

Elizabeth squeezed his hand. "Me too."

His chest still ached, but it was bearable now. Darcy looked forward to telling Anne stories of her mother, to sneaking her into the pantry to discover which pastry she favored, and to witness her grow

FITZWILLIAM DARCY, GUARDIAN

into a young woman Georgiana would be proud of. There was so much to look forward to in the years to come, the past lost some of its sting. Darcy had kept his promise, and now it was up to him to live up to the expectations that went along with it. He would do his best.

Wickham's signature was still in his pocket, and after the evening's entertainments had subsided (and the Gardiners had returned to the inn and Madame Givenchy had retired to her room) Darcy slipped away to his study. Opening his safe, he placed the precious document inside and closed it just as there was a knock on his door.

"Come in," he said, sitting behind his desk.

It was Evelyn.

"Mrs. Darcy sent me. She wanted me to give you this. She said you would get the point," the lady's maid said, bobbing a curtsy and departing before he could properly see what she had placed on the desk.

A glint of green caught Darcy's eye.

It was Elizabeth's hat pin.

EPILOGUE

THREE MONTHS LATER

*E*lizabeth rested her hand over her stomach, sipping her tea and taking in the endearing scene on the other side of her bedchamber window. It was one of the rare, brilliant days that invade winter, promising warmer months and spring flowers. William was trying to teach Anne to walk in the rose garden, holding her up by the hands as her legs wobbled and swayed between his feet. If Elizabeth listened hard, she could hear his praise and encouragement.

William made an excellent father.

Sighing contentedly, Elizabeth picked up her quill and wrote.

. . .

DEAR JANE,

We were delighted to hear of your engagement to Mr. Bingley! You will make a happy couple, I am certain of it. William agrees, and so it must be true. He is an excellent judge of character, and I am pleased he thinks so highly of my dearest sister.

Pray tell Father we will be away when he proposed to visit Pemberley. Since the news of Anne has spread, we have had several visits from William's family. As I told you in a previous letter, the Matlocks were lovely. However, I cannot say the same of his aunt Lady Catherine de Bourgh. But that is for another, lengthier letter.

What I will say is that we are in desperate need of a family outing, and William has proposed a trip to the Matlocks' nearby estate. I would have preferred the coast, but William will hear nothing of it. I suppose I ought to be grateful he is allowing me to travel at all. I shall not be able to venture far once my confinement becomes noticeable, so we really must go now if we are to go at all. I will write to Father when we return to make arrangements. If his remorse is satisfactory, perhaps we shall make amends, too.

Anne is growing more beautiful every day. I cannot wait for you to meet her, Jane. She is absolutely perfect *and so intelligent. I suspect that any day, she will say her first word. Oh, the conversations we shall have! Right now, William is showing her how to walk. It is the sweetest thing you could see and gives me the most marvelous glimpse into how happy we shall be as our family grows.*

Mrs. Reynolds is decided that our first child shall be a girl. I would never contradict her, but I know — I do not know how, but I know it all the same — that it is a boy. My dreams are full of names worthy of our son. Too bad Knightly is a surname.

Speaking of heroes and villains ... I am including a newspaper clipping from this morning's paper. It is not one to be missed. Lady Priscilla has remarried — to an Italian count, no less — and she has badgered Mr. Wickham so much, the poor, tormented soul means to leave England for good. I am glad you never had occasion to meet that horrible man. I do find it ironic he chose to flee to Australia. Vile serpent that he is, he will feel welcome surrounded by the country's enormous snakes. Maybe one will eat him. One can hope...

A TAP INTERRUPTED Elizabeth's thoughts, and she looked up to see William enter her room with Anne in his arms.

"She made a step mostly on her own today," he

said with immense pride. "We came to see if you would like to go with us for a drive."

Elizabeth stood and kissed Anne's chubby cheek. "It is too lovely a day to waste indoors. I would love to join you."

Anne squealed and squashed her face against William, shocking them both when she clearly said, "Dada."

William's chin quivered. He grinned as widely as he had the day Elizabeth had told him she loved him; as he had when she had told him she was with child. Come to think of it, William had been smiling a lot lately.

They cheered for Anne, as parents do. Elizabeth cherished the moment. She had many moments to cherish with William and a lifetime more to anticipate. They loved each other. They were happy. Their family was growing, and with it, their love and happiness would abound yet more. What they no longer had were secrets. Those were banned from the Darcy household.

No longer did Elizabeth look back on the events leading to her marriage with resentment when she could not imagine her life any other way.

Over the past three months, she had made thousands of promises — promises to William, to Anne, to her unborn child, to herself. Some spoken, some whispered in her heart. All of which she intended to keep. Time was a gift, and every day spent together was a blessing.

William had lived up to his vows. Elizabeth was confident he always would. She trusted him.

Lady Gwendolyn could keep her Sir Knightly. Elizabeth loved Fitzwilliam Darcy — the keeper of promises, the guardian of her heart.

THANK YOU!

Thank you for reading *Fitzwilliam Darcy, Guardian*! Your support and feedback make the creation of these stories possible. I'd love to know what you thought of it, so please leave a review — I read all of them.

Want to know when my next book is available? You can:

* sign up for my newsletter at www.jenniferjoy-writes.com
* follow me on twitter at @JenJoywrites
* friend my Facebook page at facebook.com/JenJoywrites
* follow my Author page on Amazon at amazon.-com/author/jenniferjoy

ABOUT THE AUTHOR

When Jennifer isn't busy dreaming up new adventures for her favorite characters, she is learning Sign language, reading, baking (Cake is her one weakness!), or chasing her twins around the park (because … calories).

She believes in happy endings, sweet romance, and plenty of mystery. She also believes there's enough angst on the news, so she keeps her stories light-hearted and full of hope.

While she claims Oregon as her home, she currently lives high in the Andes Mountains of Ecuador with her husband and two kids.

Written in the Stars: Starlight Terrace Proposals, Novella 1

Made in the USA
Columbia, SC
04 December 2019